# LIGHT OF THE WITCH
## A WITCHES OF KEATING HOLLOW NOVELLA

KEATING HOLLOW HAPPILY EVER AFTERS
BOOK THREE

DEANNA CHASE

read the title out loud. "*The Witch of Redwood Grove* by Maeve Woods. Huh. Why don't I recognize this one?"

Poppy ran over to the reading area and sat in the front with her cousins.

Yvette flipped to the back to read the author's bio. It was short and to the point.

*Maeve Woods has a soft spot for magic and was inspired to write this book by her niece. This is her first book.* The publication date was five years earlier. Yvette couldn't believe the book had been on the shelf for five years and she hadn't ever noticed it. That was very unlike her. Especially a children's book as they did read-alongs every week. She was about to ask Brinn, her assistant, about it, but the other woman was busy helping someone else find the travel section.

It didn't matter anyway. At least she got to read a new-to-her book that afternoon.

"Yvette!" Abby, one of her sisters, called. "Let's get this show on the road so we can get the kids out of here before dinnertime."

"Sure." Yvette smirked at her younger sister. While no one wanted to deal with hungry kids, Yvette knew Abby was equally as concerned about getting sisters' night started. After the reading, the dads were taking the kids while Yvette, Abby, Noel, Faith, and Hope went out for a little sister time. It wasn't often that the five of them got to spend uninterrupted quality time together, so Yvette couldn't blame Abby for her excitement.

"Okay, who wants to help me read *The Witch of Redwood Grove?*" Yvette asked.

Poppy jumped up and ran to Yvette's side before any of the other kids could even raise their hands.

Yvette stifled a chuckle. "Okay, I suppose it's your turn anyway."

Her niece nodded vigorously. "Toby read last week, and the week before it was Lynette."

"Sure, she remembers that," Noel muttered. "But she never remembers to put the cap on the toothpaste."

Poppy stuck her tongue out at her mother and then opened the book. With Yvette's help, she proceeded to read about a witch who lived in the woods and was hired to cast an abundance spell.

When it came time to read the spell aloud, Yvette took over, using a dramatic voice that made the kids giggle. *"Goddess of the redwoods, bring peace and harmony and abundance to the people of Redwood Grove."*

As Poppy read on, it soon became clear that the spell had backfired due to the witch's impure heart. Instead of abundance, everyone in town had something to struggle with. It turned out that in order for the spell to be reversed, the witch had to let go of her bitterness and learn to love again. That love came in the form of a sweet, abandoned puppy who needed a home. In the end, the witch named her puppy Love Bug and the people in the town began to flourish.

"Love Bug!" Toby called. "I want a puppy named Love Bug!"

Yvette looked at her son and gave him a patient smile.

"Yeah, we should get a golden retriever," Skye chimed in.

Stifling a groan, Yvette caught her husband Jacob's eye and gave him a half shrug. He'd have to handle this one.

"We'll talk about it later," Jacob said, wrapping an arm around both Skye and Toby.

Yvette's two kids chattered excitedly about a puppy, and she decided then and there if they wanted a dog it was fine with her. But only if Jacob was willing to train the thing. There just weren't enough hours in the day for Yvette to run the bookstore and train a puppy.

Jacob steered the kids toward Yvette and then whispered something to both of them. They immediately dislodged from their dad and gave her a group hug. He winked and then leaned in and kissed her on the cheek. "Have fun tonight."

"You, too," she said and watched with a heart full of love as they made their way out of the store.

"Need help closing up?" Abby asked as the rest of the kids and dads filed out of the store.

"Sure." Yvette directed her sister to clean up the refreshment area while she closed out the register.

"I'll vacuum," Noel said, already heading for the back room to get the appliance.

Faith and Hope both helped straighten up the kid's area while Yvette ran the sales report for the day. Once she had it in hand, she stared down at the numbers and blinked. Had she done the report correctly? The number was lower than their worst day ever. She decided to run it again.

The number was the same.

Had she been dreaming when she saw all the other kids in the shop for the read-along? They hadn't all been her family, had they? No, definitely not.

She quickly counted the cash in the register and closed out the credit card terminal. While the day's haul was incredibly disappointing, she just chalked it up to one bad day. They happened, right?

Though usually not on a read-along day when the store was packed. And definitely not in the spring when Keating Hollow had a ton of tourists and all the residents were out and about enjoying the lovely warm weather.

"Are you about ready, Yvette?" Abby called from her place by the front door. She had her long blond hair pulled up into a bun and was chomping on a leftover pumpkin scone from Incantation Café. Noel was sitting in one of the overstuffed velvet chairs, riffling through a regional travel magazine. One glimpse told Yvette it was the one that had Noel's inn advertised on the back cover.

Hope and Faith were in their own world, chatting about the spa where they both worked.

"Yep." Yvette dropped the day's minuscule haul into the safe and locked the register. A one-off day was nothing to worry about. "Let's get this party started."

"Excellent." Abby held the front door open for her sisters. "The golf cart is ready to go."

Abby hadn't been kidding. The twinkling lights that covered the golf cart were lit, and there was already music blaring from the aftermarket speakers.

"I hope there are margaritas in that cooler," Yvette said, eyeing the back of the golf cart.

"You bet." Abby grinned. "Get in."

Abby took the wheel with Yvette in the front seat, while the other three sisters sat behind them. "Get the Party Started" by P!nk blared from the speakers as Abby put the pedal to the metal and steered them toward Keating Hollow's magical river.

The five of them sang at the top of their lungs, burning off steam as the cool spring air whipped through their hair. Yvette hadn't felt that free in a long time. With the pressures of motherhood and running a small business, it was often hard to find time just for herself. The sister time Abby had organized for the night was exactly what she needed.

The moon was full, shimmering off the river that ran through the town. With the redwoods lining the other side, it made Yvette feel as if they'd just wandered into the woods, even though they were just a few minutes from Main Street.

Abby came to a stop, turned the music down, and asked, "Who needs a drink?"

"Me!" all of the other four sisters said at once.

Yvette chuckled and got up to help Abby pour the margaritas from the gallon thermos that was tucked into the cooler. Once they all had a drink in their hand, they walked over to the large fallen tree that had been used as a bench for many years.

"Where's Wanda?" Hope asked. "A golf cart race would be just the thing to cap off the night."

Abby laughed. "Yeah, I thought about that, but tonight... I don't know. I thought it would be nice if it was just the five of us, you know? We never spend time together when it isn't with the husbands and kids."

"I think this is perfect," Noel said as she rose from the trunk and moved to lie in the grass so she could look up at the stars.

Faith downed her drink and then followed Noel's lead. "Agreed. I love Wanda, but this feels soul restoring."

Yvette and Abby shared a glance. It was exactly why they hadn't invited Wanda or Hanna or any of their other friends in town. Life had proven to be very busy for all of them. and for once, they just wanted an opportunity to slow down a bit.

"Look!" Noel pointed to the sky. "It's a shooting star."

Yvette glanced up and let out a surprised gasp. Shooting stars started to fill the sky, one after another.

"Quick! Make a wish!" Abby cried as she took her spot on the grass next to Faith.

Yvette gestured for Hope to join her, and soon all five sisters were lined up, staring at the unexpected phenomenon in the sky.

It wasn't long before Abby reached for Yvette's hand and Yvette reached for Hope's. Yvette knew without asking that Abby also had Faith's hand and Faith had Noel's. There was a magical spark that lit up inside of Yvette when all five sisters connected. It made her feel both peaceful and powerful. There was nothing more potent than family.

"Everyone think of their wish," Abby whispered.

Yvette concentrated on the shooting stars in the sky, felt the magic pulsing from her sisters around her, and imagined her and Jacob enjoying some quiet time together. Possibly a drive in the mountains or an overnight trip in a quaint nearby town where the two of them could spend some time reconnecting away from the pressures of parenthood and work.

A sense of calm washed over her, and she got a flash of her and Jacob in her SUV, following the river deep into the mountains. The sun was casting dappled light on the two-lane road, and everything about the scene looked peaceful and serene. She smiled to herself at the premonition and hoped the trip would be soon.

"So mote it be," Abby said.

Yvette and her three other sisters echoed Abby's words. "So mote it be."

"Okay." Abby sat up and started refilling everyone's margarita glasses.

When everyone had a fresh drink except for Abby, Yvette asked, "Where's yours?"

Abby shook her head. "Someone has to drive you drunks home. Since I'm already in the driver's seat, I guess it's me." She gave them all a wicked grin and asked, "Who's in for a round of Truth or Dare?"

Yvette groaned. "The last time we played that, I ended up running naked through the woods."

Abby slapped her hands together with glee. "I know. And I'll never forget when the neighbor's nephew wolf-whistled and offered his hand in marriage. Too bad you didn't accept. You could have been Yvette Boner, and instead of running a bookstore, you would've been the heir to the Barely There Underwear empire."

Hope sputtered on her margarita. "You can't be serious."

"Maaaannn," Abby said. "I hate that you missed out on our shenanigans when we were younger. Our mother deserves extra prison time for depriving you of that day."

Yvette snorted sardonically. Their mother had up and

left town when her four daughters with Lincoln Townsend were still young. It turned out she'd had an affair and was pregnant with Hope. Because of a potions addiction, she'd given Hope up for adoption, and the four Townsend sisters hadn't even known Hope existed until eight years ago when she was twenty years old. Now Gabrielle Townsend was serving a prison sentence for using a forbidden curse that had endangered Abby and her family. All of the Townsend sisters had filed restraining orders for the day when she was eventually paroled.

"I'm sure there are plenty of other awful reasons why she should stay locked up," Hope muttered.

"No doubt," Noel chimed in.

There was silence among the sisters until Yvette said, "Enough Mom talk. Abby, truth or dare?"

Abby narrowed her eyes and said, "Dare."

Yvette gave her an evil grin and said, "I dare you to run naked into the river."

"Is that the best you can do?" Abby rolled her eyes and started to strip. Once she was skyclad, she bolted for the river.

Yvette, who already had her phone ready, snapped a picture of her sister's lily-white backside and quickly texted it to Clay, Abby's husband, with the caption *Your wife is out of control.*

*Isn't she always?* He texted back almost immediately.

The sisters cackled, their laughter echoing off the river.

"What's so funny?" Abby called from where she was bobbing in the water.

Yvette waved her phone at her. "You're a porn star now."

They were still laughing when Abby returned, quickly got dressed, and said, "Your turn, Yvette."

Yvette swallowed hard and awaited her punishment.

Two hours later, with an empty thermos of margaritas and aches in their sides from laughing too hard, Abby drove her sisters home.

Yvette stumbled up the stairs to her house on the side of the mountain and waved as Abby honked and then darted out of her driveway.

"Looks like someone had fun," Jacob said from the doorway.

Yvette turned around to see her handsome, dark-haired husband smiling at her with that sexy half grin she loved so much. She took a step forward, stumbled, and found herself in his arms, right where she wanted to be. "Not as much fun as we're about to have."

He chuckled softly. "Is that right? Just how drunk are you?"

"Drunk enough to charm the pants off you, not drunk enough not to know what I'm doing," she said and then hiccuped.

"Sure, 'Vette," he said softly as he shook his head, clearly amused. "If you make it to the bedroom, I'll let you do more than charm the pants off me."

"You bet you will." She pushed past him, stumbled again, and then used the wall to right herself.

"Never mind. You'll wake the kids if you keep that up." Jacob scooped her up in his arms, kicked the door shut, and carried her to the bedroom.

The last thing she remembered before passing out was her head hitting the pillow as he laid her gently on the bed.

## CHAPTER 2

*J*acob paused in the doorway of his bedroom and smirked at his wife, Yvette.

"Please tell me that coffee is for me," she said as she squinted at him, her brows pinched together.

"It is for you," he said as he walked over and sat gingerly beside her. "I considered making you breakfast, but I'm guessing you're going to need a minute to get your sea legs."

"Oh. My. Goddess. Do not talk about food or the sea right now," she said with a moan.

"Is it that bad?" He set the coffee mug on the nightstand and ran a soft thumb over her forehead.

"Yes. Abby makes strong margaritas, and all I had for dinner was a pastry." She pushed herself up so that she was leaning against the headboard. "Next time remind me that I'm not twenty-two anymore."

"You still look twenty-two," he said.

"You're a liar. And stop flashing those dimples at me. You're annoyingly handsome this morning while I'm sure I look like a troll." She reached for the coffee and let out a contented sigh when she realized he'd made her a latte. "Annoying, but a god among men."

Jacob chuckled softly. "A god might be a little much, but I'll take husband of the year."

"Done." She took a long sip of the latte and let out a sigh of relief. "That's exactly what I needed. I might actually live."

"That's good to hear." Jacob leaned over and kissed her on the temple. "I'll go make you some toast."

"And fried eggs?" she asked hopefully. "Over easy?"

"You got it." He was still smiling as he headed to the kitchen.

∽

JACOB SAT AT HIS DESK, staring at the blank page of chapter three of his manuscript. Even though he had an outline for the midgrade novel he was writing, he just couldn't get this chapter started.

After years of working in the book business, Jacob had finally decided he wanted to be on the creative end instead of the retail end. And since he and Yvette had decided that he'd be the one to stay home as the primary caregiver for their kids, he finally had time to write. Or at least he did when the kids were at school and he wasn't struggling with writer's block.

His phone vibrated on the desk, and when he picked it up, he saw Yvette's smiling face. "Hi gorgeous," he said as he answered.

"That never gets old," she said with a small sigh.

"Feeling better?" he asked.

"Much. It's helped that it's been really slow this morning. I was able to take it easy and knock this headache out. Brinn brought me another latte and a coffee cake from Incantation Café. I think the sugar helped."

Jacob glanced out the window at the brilliant blue sky. "Good thing. You'll probably be slammed this afternoon."

"We usually are on Fridays. I just wanted to call and say hi before we get busy. And to thank you for breakfast."

"You don't have to thank me," Jacob said, his chest warming with affection. "I'm happy to do it."

"I know. That's why you're both the sweetest and most annoying husband in the world," she teased. "You make me look bad."

He laughed. "If you say so."

Yvette blew him a kiss over the phone and then ended the call.

Jacob took another look out at the gorgeous day and decided that he needed a change of scenery. If he wasn't feeling inspired in his office, maybe he'd do better in town. He closed his laptop, grabbed his keys, and headed for the Toyota Sequoia parked in the driveway.

Fifteen minutes later, he parked in the nearly empty parking lot of the Keating Hollow Brewery. He glanced at the time on his phone, making sure he hadn't arrived before they opened. But when he saw it was just after noon, he frowned. Normally there'd be quite the lunch crowd by now. But considering he was going in to grab lunch and work, maybe it was exactly what he needed.

The brewery was indeed dead. There wasn't anyone in the place except for Rhys and Hanna. Rhys, the assistant brewer, was behind the bar, and his wife, Hanna, was sitting across from him. Rhys raised his hand in greeting.

Jacob nodded to him and made his way to the bar. He took a seat next to Hanna and said, "Hey, you two. How's it going?"

Rhys glanced around the pub and said, "Kinda slow."

"Kinda?" Hanna asked with a snort. "I left the café early since there's nothing to do."

"Seriously?" Jacob asked. "Yvette said the bookstore is

slow, too. Is Caltrans working on the highway or something?"

There were two ways in and out of Keating Hollow. One was the two-lane highway out to the coast, and the other was the two-lane highway up into the mountains. Hardly anyone came into Keating Hollow via the mountains. If there was a problem, it would be on the road that led to the coast.

"That's a thought," Rhys said. "I bet Drew would know."

Jacob nodded and pulled out his phone to call his brother-in-law, who was the town sheriff.

"Jacob, what's up?" Drew asked after he answered the call.

"Do you know if there's road work on the highway from Eureka or an accident maybe that's holding up traffic?" Jacob asked.

"Haven't heard anything," Drew said. Jacob heard the sound of a keyboard clacking before Drew added, "I don't see any reports in the online system either."

"Okay, that's good to know." Jacob shook his head, letting Rhys know there wasn't any roadwork happening.

"Why?" Drew asked.

"Just wondering what's going on. Main Street is a ghost town right now. Seems odd for this time of year, especially on a Friday."

Drew let out a huff of laughter. "It's likely the calm

before the storm. You watch. Just because you said that, town is going to be packed to the gills this weekend. Enjoy the quiet while you can."

"Will do." Jacob relayed the message to Rhys and Hanna.

Hanna grimaced. "He's probably right, and tomorrow is going to be hell."

"But at least you'll have a full pocketbook," Rhys said with a wink.

"One can only hope." Hanna picked up the burger that was in front of her and took a giant bite.

"That's my girl," Rhys said, egging her on.

Jacob ordered a beer and a burger of his own and then took his laptop to a table to get to work.

The change of pace did the trick, and before he knew it, he was finishing the chapter he'd had so much trouble with back in his office. He was just about to go pay his bill when Rhys yelled, "Jacob! Help!"

Jacob rushed over to the bar, where he found Rhys struggling with a tap that was gushing beer. "What can I do?" Jacob asked.

"Hold this tap up while I go shut down the keg."

Jacob did as he was asked, doing his best to keep the tap from spewing beer. As he was standing there, a second tap started gushing. He grabbed that one, trying to get it to stop, but nothing he tried worked. "Rhys, hurry up!"

"I've almost got it!" Rhys called back from the nearby room that housed the kegs.

"Rhys!" he shouted again. Now both taps had turned into geysers, and there was nothing Jacob could do to stop the flow.

"I've got it!" Rhys cried as he reappeared.

But before Jacob could say anything, all the remaining taps exploded, and Jacob found himself drenched in beer from head to toe.

"Holy hell," Rhys said as he stared in awed horror at the scene.

Jacob stopped struggling with the taps and backed away until he was no longer under the spray of beer. After wiping the liquid from his eyes, he glanced around at the destruction and just blinked.

"What the hell happened?" Clay Garrison asked when he suddenly appeared from the brewhouse behind the bar.

"The taps exploded," Jacob said. "Do you think I could get a towel?"

"I'll get it," Rhys said and disappeared.

Clay stared at the destruction. "Did a witch come in and blow everything up?"

"That's a great theory. Too bad there was no one else in here except for me and Rhys. Hanna left about a half hour ago," Jacob said.

Clay scratched the back of his head, looking confused. "I don't understand. Taps don't just explode like that."

"I don't know, man," Jacob said as Rhys returned and handed him a towel. "But the evidence is all over me."

"Damn, sorry about that, Jacob," Clay said.

"Not your fault." Jacob quickly toweled off as much as possible and then handed the towel back to Rhys. "I'd stick around and try to help you determine a cause, but I have to go pick up the kids from school. Talk to you both later."

"Later," Clay said, already sounding distracted as he moved toward the taps that were now just trickling beer.

Jacob grabbed his laptop and cursed as he looked down at himself. Driving around in wet, beer-soaked clothes sounded miserable, but there was no time to go home and change.

He hurried to his SUV, jumped in, and took off toward the school. When he was only two blocks away, a siren sounded just as lights flashed behind him. "What the—"

Jacob pulled over, expecting the cruiser to fly right by, but he was surprised when the cop car pulled up behind him.

He ground his teeth and waited for what seemed like forever for the police officer to come to his window. Jacob was about ready to jump out of the SUV to see what the holdup was when a short, skinny man with a severely receding hairline approached the window.

"You're lucky you didn't hit anyone the way you sped through that stop sign," the police officer said.

"Stop sign?" Jacob asked. "What are you talking about?"

"The new one the city just put in yesterday. You just rolled right through it." He gestured to the intersection right behind them. "That's gonna cost ya." The officer raised his chin and sniffed. Then he narrowed his eyes at Jacob. "Just how much beer did you have with lunch, Mister?"

"Just one. About two hours ago," Jacob said, annoyed. "I drive this route every day to pick up my kids—"

"Pick up your kids? No, sir. Not in your condition. Please get out of the vehicle," the policeman ordered.

"What?"

"Sir, step out of the vehicle. Now!"

Jacob sucked in a deep breath and did as he was told. The minute he shut the Toyota's door, the police officer slapped cuffs on him and started reading him his rights.

"Why are you arresting me?" Jacob demanded.

"For driving under the influence. Keep talking, buddy. It's only going to get you a longer sentence."

"You haven't even given me a breathalyzer," Jacob said. "You can't arrest me."

"I can, and I will. Now get in the cruiser." The man

pushed Jacob into the back seat of his cruiser and then jumped in, his lights and siren still going as he sped back to the police station.

Jacob was fuming but chose to keep his comments to himself. There was no point in arguing with the man. Once he was at the station, he knew his brother-in-law would straighten everything out.

When they arrived, the officer pulled Jacob from the back of the car and pushed him toward the front door. "Hurry up. The sooner we get inside, the sooner I can throw you in the drunk tank."

"That sounds pleasant," Jacob said dryly.

"Shut up." The officer pulled the door open and shoved Jacob into the building.

Drew Baker looked up from a file he was studying and blinked at Jacob. "What in the world? Jacob?"

"This man recklessly ran the new stop sign, and when I pulled him over to give him a warning, he smelled of beer so badly it nearly got me drunk just breathing the air around him."

"Because the taps blew up at the Keating Hollow Brewery, and I was trying to help Rhys before they lost all of them. I got drenched in beer, but I only drank one glass with lunch, and that was over two hours ago," Jacob said.

"Deputy Crooks," Drew said, narrowing his eyes at

the officer still gripping Jacob's arm. "What is this man's blood alcohol level?"

"Well... I... I didn't think I needed to bother with that considering—"

"Uncuff him now, Crooks. And then go wait in my office."

"But—"

"That's an order, Crooks."

The deputy grumbled under this breath while he took his time unlocking the handcuffs. But then he slunk away, looking like a dog with his tail between his legs.

"Drew, I need to call Yvette. The kids are waiting to be picked up from school," Jacob said.

"I'll have Noel get them," Drew said as he held his phone up to his ear. "She'll be there picking up Daisy and Poppy anyway, and I want to hear exactly what happened today."

Jacob shrugged and then slumped into a hard plastic chair. "Sure. Why not."

Drew got Noel on the phone, and she promised to pick up Jacob and Yvette's kids and to call Yvette to let her know what happened.

"Tell her thanks," Jacob mumbled, more miserable than ever in his still-damp clothes.

Once he'd finished the call, Drew sat next to Jacob and said, "Sorry about that. Crooks is new."

"He needs to be put on leave until he figures out how to do his job," Jacob grumbled.

"Believe me, he will be reprimanded," Drew said. "Now come with me. I want to make an official report."

Jacob sighed and followed his brother-in-law, wondering when exactly the day had turned to crap. Right about the time he'd had a beer shower, he decided, chuckling to himself.

"What's so funny?" Drew asked.

"The term *beer shower*," Jacob said. "There was a time in my life when I'd have welcomed such an event. But today? Now I'm running carpool and writing at a pub instead of holding up the bar."

Drew smiled at him as they took seats in his office. "One day you're just an average dude with no responsibilities and a fridge full of beer, and the next you're running carpool."

Jacob laughed. "True. Who could have imagined?"

"Not me, but here we are." He pulled out a notebook and said, "Okay, tell me everything."

Jacob took a deep breath and dove in.

## CHAPTER 3

"What happened to you?" Yvette asked when Jacob walked in the door smelling like a brewery. All she knew was that Noel had picked up the kids and that Jacob was with Drew, but she didn't know why. All her calls to his phone had gone straight to voice mail. "And why didn't you call me back?"

"My phone is dead." He placed it on the coffee table in front of her, showing the black screen. He glanced around. "Where are the kids?"

"In Skye's room. They're playing a game and talking about what kind of dog they want." Yvette stood and went over to her husband despite the fumes. "I think you need a shower."

"There's no doubt about that. But first I could really use a cup of coffee. It's been one heck of a day."

"You go to the shower. I'll get the coffee," Yvette said, wrinkling her nose. Besides the scent, she wasn't excited for the kids to see their father looking so disheveled after he'd no-showed to pick them up from school.

"Thanks."

While Jacob disappeared into the bedroom, Yvette made his coffee and then went to wait for him.

When he emerged in a fresh pair of jeans with wet hair, she handed him the mug.

Jacob took a long swig and then said, "You're a lifesaver."

Yvette curled up in a chair and waited for him to fill her in.

"I was arrested for drunk driving," he blurted before sitting on the end of the bed, looking like he wanted to sleep for a week.

Yvette sat up straight, hardly believing her ears. "You were… drunk? While picking up the kids?!"

"No. I had one beer with lunch, two hours before I left the brewery." He went on to explain the tap explosion and then how he'd run a newly installed stop sign. "The cop, some dude named Crooks, arrested me without even testing my blood alcohol level."

"Crooks? Who's that?" Yvette asked, trying to place the man. Keating Hollow was a small town. Everyone pretty much knew everyone else.

"Some new guy. Drew was pissed and wrote him up

for not following procedure. Then we had to get the Sequoia out of impound before I could get home. The paperwork..." He shook his head. "And with my phone dead, I didn't know you were calling. I thought Noel would fill you in."

Yvette shook her head. "She said she hadn't had time to get any details from Drew as she was dealing with her own crisis. A wedding party canceled last minute, and she had to call all the vendors to let them know the wedding was off. It sounds like a nightmare. So now, not only is she not getting the rest of the wedding fee, but her inn is empty for the weekend, too."

"That's awful. And the brewery is going to be out of commission while they get the taps fixed." Jacob downed the rest of his coffee. "Is it Friday the 13$^{th}$ or something? Seems like there's some serious bad luck going around."

Yvette slumped back into her chair. "I guess I'll stop complaining about slow sales. At least nothing exploded. Our only issue is that we only sold a couple of books today. And Hanna bought those when she stopped by to drop off pastries for the coffee bar this morning."

"Maybe the issue is the canceled wedding," Jacob offered. "If they were filling the inn, that would explain the lack of tourists."

"Partly, maybe, but Keating Hollow still has a lot of short-term rentals. Seems unlikely all of those would have been for the wedding, but I suppose it's possible."

Yvette's phone buzzed. She glanced down to see a text chain that included all her sisters.

The first message was from Faith. *A pipe burst at the spa. Out of commission for the foreseeable future. Heavy sigh.*

It was followed by a response from Abby. *Are the Townsends cursed? The brewery's taps are down, and it'll be a week at least before we can get the right parts to get them up and running again.*

*I think we are,* Hope chimed in. *Chad's music store was broken into last night. Thousands of dollars of inventory was stolen or destroyed. It's devastating.*

Noel replied with the troubles at the inn next.

Yvette stared at her phone, unable to comprehend what was happening. "I think we *have* been cursed," she said, still staring at the phone.

"Why do you think that?" Jacob asked as he rose and pulled on a T-shirt.

She handed him the phone so he could read for himself. Frowning, he looked up. "Why would anyone curse us? And who?"

"That's the million-dollar question, isn't it?" Yvette took her phone back and tapped out her own message. *Emergency meeting at Dad's? Half hour? Something's seriously wrong, and we need to get to the bottom of this.*

The replies were swift. Every Townsend sister would be there.

"We're going to need a lot of pizza," Jacob said.

Yvette nodded, texted that they'd take care of dinner, and asked Abby to let their dad know he was being invaded.

*On it!* Abby texted back.

～

LESS THAN AN HOUR LATER, Jacob drove up the tree-lined drive that led to the Townsend family home. Twinkle lights shone from each of the trees, and it looked just as magical as it always did. Yvette was in the passenger seat, and the kids were in the back. They parked behind a line of cars, and before they could all climb out of the vehicle, Clay and Drew were there to unload the pizzas.

Yvette herded her kids into the house and then out to the backyard where all their cousins were hanging out with Clair, her father's fiancée. And when Silas and Levi showed up right after she did, all the kids ran over to them, not caring at all that the two men were big-time famous movie and rock stars. All they cared about was the fact that their uncles were back in town.

"I didn't know you guys were here," Yvette said to Levi. "Did you just get back in town?"

Levi nodded. "Hope told me what's going on, and we decided to come by and help keep the kids occupied so you all can meet without interruptions." Levi was Hope's half brother, and as far as the Townsends were concerned, he'd been folded into the family just like Hope had been. Silas was his fiancé.

"Thank you!" Yvette threw her arms around Levi and blew Silas a kiss. "You two are incredible, you know that, right?"

Levi let out an embarrassed chuckle. "Just trying to help."

Yvette kissed him on the cheek. "There's pizza in the kitchen, and don't be afraid to come get any of us if the kids get out of line, okay?"

"We've got it," Silas said and winked at her. Then he got a serious expression on his face when he said, "Go on in. It sounds like you all have a lot to discuss."

"Yeah," she said with a sigh and headed back inside. She found Jacob sitting at the end of the couch holding a plate with two slices of her favorite pizza and a diet soda. She gave him a grateful smile and sat on the arm of the couch, leaving room for her siblings.

Lincoln Townsend walked into the room just as everyone settled in. They all had pizza, but no one was really eating it. After the day they'd had, no one was particularly hungry.

"It appears we have a problem," Lincoln said. "Is there anyone here who hasn't seen their business suffer a major event?"

Yvette raised her hand as she looked around at all her sisters and their husbands. No one else had their hand in the air. She cleared her throat. "Business has been nonexistent the last couple of days, but other than that, the store is fine. No break-ins and no flooding at least." She grimaced as she looked at Faith and tried not to imagine her beloved spa soaked with water.

"No exploding taps?" Abby asked.

"Nope. The espresso machine was just fine when I left it today," Yvette said, referring to the coffee bar section of the bookstore. "No smashed inventory. No event cancellations. Am I missing anything?"

Hunter, Faith's husband, cleared his throat. "On the way over, I got a call that the custom home we're building collapsed." He was a contractor and had become one of the town's go-to builders. If word of this got out, people would be hesitant to hire him for future jobs.

Yvette sucked in a sharp breath as she pressed her palm to her chest. "Is everyone all right?"

He nodded. "Luckily the crew had already left for the day, but it needs to be rebuilt from the ground up."

"What happened? Do you know?" Lincoln asked him.

Hunter's face was full of fury as he spit out, "Deliberate sabotage. A major support beam was cut with a chain saw."

"Who is doing all this?" Hope asked as she stood and paced the living room. "Every single one of our small businesses have been targeted."

"I'd say that Gabrielle hired someone on the outside

to target us," Yvette said. "But that doesn't explain the wedding cancellation or the lack of tourists in Keating Hollow."

"Yeah, my lotions and potions business hasn't seen a single sale in two days," Abby added. "And that includes my online store. That's just... unheard of. How could she have sabotaged that?"

"It could have been a spell," Noel said. "She could have had us cursed. She's done it before."

Lincoln shook his head. "She can't cast from prison. And it would cost a lot of money to pay someone to do it for her. Money she doesn't have. Besides, your mother has often made terrible choices, but she has never been purely spiteful. Even the last spell she cast was just to get Abby's attention. This..." He waved his hand around the room. "It's something else entirely."

Yvette wasn't so sure she agreed with her father. Gabrielle was in prison for using illegal spells. If the experience had exacerbated her bitterness, anything was possible. She stood and said, "Maybe one of us should go see her and find out."

"Not it!" Abby said, a surly expression on her face.

"I'm not going either," Noel chimed in.

"I barely even know her," Hope said.

Yvette met Faith's gaze.

Faith gave her a tiny shake of the head. "I have enough

on my plate. Dealing with her might be the straw that breaks the camel's back."

Yvette nodded, understanding completely. Faith had triplets and now had to deal with a flooded business. She sighed. "I guess that leaves me."

"If you go, I'll go with you," Lincoln said.

"Thanks, Dad. That's—" Suddenly something on the mantel started to glow with shimmering magic. "What in the world is that?"

Lincoln walked over and plucked the object off the mantle. As soon as he touched it, the magic vanished and he was left holding a book.

A children's book.

*The Witch of Redwood Grove.*

## CHAPTER 4

"How did that get here?" Yvette exclaimed, every fiber of her being on full alert. That was the book she'd read the day before at the read-along. "Did one of the kids bring it?"

"I have no idea." Lincoln frowned at the cover. "I've never even heard of this before." With the book still clutched in his hand, he walked out of the living room and into the kitchen.

Yvette followed him as he stepped outside.

Lincoln walked over to Clair, who was busy tying Toby's shoe. Once she was done, he asked, "Have you seen this book before?"

She studied the book, frowned, and then shook her head. "No. Where did you find it?"

"On the mantel. Glowing with magic," Yvette chimed in.

Clair blinked rapidly as she processed the information. "That's unusual."

"You can say that again," Lincoln said.

"All the children's books are kept in the playroom," Clair said. "And the cleaning service was just here yesterday. Peggy wouldn't have left that out. So unless one of the children moved it, I don't see how it got there."

Yvette made her way through the kids, asking each of them if they'd brought the book. They all said no.

When she got to Poppy, Noel's little girl looked positively upset. "I put that back on your shelf, Aunt Yvette. I swear I didn't steal it!"

"No one is accusing you of stealing anything, sweet pea," Yvette soothed. "I'm just trying to solve the puzzle of how it got here. That's all. No one is in trouble."

Relief washed over the little girl's face, followed by a frown. "Where's the broom?"

"What broom?" Yvette asked.

"The one that was on the cover yesterday." Poppy pointed to the illustrated witch who was standing next to a cobblestone cottage. "She had a broom in her hand, and there was magic swirling around it."

Yvette tried to remember what the cover had looked like the night before, but she was coming up blank. "You're saying this is a different book?"

Poppy shrugged. "Different cover anyway."

"Okay." Yvette wasn't sure if Poppy was remembering correctly, but there was only one way to find out. She tucked the book under her arm and gave Poppy a hug. "Thanks. That's very helpful."

"It is?" Her eyes lit up from the praise before she returned the hug, squeezing Yvette so tight she coughed. When she let go, Yvette gave her niece a kiss on the cheek and gestured for Lincoln to follow her back inside.

"Any luck?" Abby asked.

"Nope," Lincoln said for both of them. "But I think it's pretty clear that book is connected to whatever curse has fallen on this family."

Yvette thought so, too. Why else would it have started glowing when they began speculating that someone had cursed them? She placed the book on the coffee table. Then she said, "Goddess of the light, we seek knowledge. Did we unknowingly unleash a curse from this book? Goddess of the light, give us the gift of sight."

The book rose from the coffee table seemingly on its own, shimmered with magic, and then suddenly fell, landing with a loud thump back onto the table. The magical light from the book stayed suspended and then swirled and spiraled, forming the word *Yes*.

Yvette sucked in a sharp breath. Even though she'd been the one to suspect the book was the problem, she was still startled. It seemed impossible, but the spell had revealed the truth.

"Oh, crap," Abby said as she slumped back against the couch.

"Now what?" Hope asked.

"We could try to break it," Noel said.

"Yes. Let's try that." Yvette picked up the book, holding onto it gingerly as if it were going to bite her.

"Where?" Abby asked.

Yvette wrinkled her nose as she thought of all the kids out back and said, "Better go out front. We need to make a pentagram."

"Let's do it." Abby popped up and led the charge out the front door.

Lincoln walked over to the desk in the corner of the room and extracted a green velvet bag from the bottom drawer. He handed it to Yvette. "You're going to need these."

She peeked in the bag, found chalk, salt, and white pillar candles. Smiling up at her father, she said, "Thanks. This will come in handy."

All of the spouses followed the sisters out to the front of the house.

Hunter was the one who took the chalk and got to work on the pentagram. Jacob joined him while Drew took the salt and made a circle around the area.

Once the pentagram was ready, each of the five sisters

stood at a point. Yvette, as the oldest, placed the book in the middle of the pentagram and then stood at the northern most point.

The heaviness of the situation weighed on Yvette. She'd been the one to read the book. The one who'd read the spell out loud and had set everything into motion. Even though she'd in no way invoked her power to cast a spell, that didn't seem to matter. Whatever magic was infused in the book had been enough. She just prayed that she and her sisters could neutralize it. It would eat her alive knowing that she was responsible for all their businesses suffering.

"We've got this, 'Vette," Abby said. "If it's possible to break this curse, we'll get it done."

Yvette wished she shared her confidence, but she nodded anyway and held the white pillar candle in front of her.

All of her sisters followed her lead. She met each of their gazes and then called, "Ignite!"

The candles all flickered to life.

Yvette let out a sigh of relief. It had been a long time since she'd led any kind of spell. She'd hoped it'd be just like riding a bike, but she hadn't been sure.

The familiar Townsend magic flickered over her skin as she said, "Elevate!"

The candles all started to float in the air in front of each of her sisters, leaving their hands free.

Yvette reached each arm out to Abby and Noel, who were on either side of her. Her sister's followed her lead until each of them had their arms spread wide and their magic pulsing from their fingers.

"Air, earth, water, fire, and spirit, the Townsend sisters call upon you to right a wrong. Combine our powers, use our strength and our will to break an unjust curse. Undo the spell. Release our energy. Banish the curse and neutralize the hold it has over us, our families, and our businesses. Return Keating Hollow to its natural order. Air, earth, water, fire, and spirit, hear our call, right a wrong, banish the curse, return Keating Hollow to the natural order!"

Magical particles sparked all around them, and then suddenly, they all came together to form a large ball of light. It hovered just over the book and then shot right into it, raising the book into the air and opening it right to the curse.

The magic formed the words of the incantation. Yvette was singularly focused when she cried, "Break the curse!"

The words shattered into hundreds of pieces of shimmering light before floating to the ground. The moment the particles hit the dirt the magic winked out.

The book slammed shut and fell once again, hitting the middle of the pentagram. A tendril of smoke rose from the book as the magic faded away into the night.

"It worked, right?" Hope asked. "It looked like it worked."

"It felt like it, too," Faith offered.

Noel and Abby shared a look with Yvette, indicating that they weren't quite sure.

"There's really only one way to find out," Yvette said.

"How's that?" Abby asked, looking at her curiously.

"Go home, get some sleep, and find out what tomorrow brings," Lincoln said, already picking up the book and the pillar candles. He was a stickler about putting things away where they belonged. Especially anything to do with magic.

Yvette glanced around at her sisters and then motioned for them to gather around her. "I pray this works," she said. "And I'm really sorry about what's already happened. No one deserves any of that."

"It's not your fault," Abby said, looking at Yvette with concern.

"I'm the one who read the spell out loud. I should've known better. With all of you in the room, I'm sure it made it even stronger."

"It's a children's book. You didn't know it was activating a spell," Abby insisted. "It could have happened to any of us. Understand?"

Yvette knew that was true. Still, it didn't stop her from feeling like she was the one to blame.

"Yvette?" Abby warned.

"I hear you," Yvette said.

"Good. Now let's get out of here. We all have a lot of work to do tomorrow."

Everyone except for Yvette. But she kept that thought to herself, nodded, and then looked at Jacob. "Ready to get the kids?"

He shook his head. "Nope. They're staying here for the night." Grinning, he added, "Grandma Clair insisted."

"Grandma Clair is a goddess," Yvette said. "Come on. Let's go say goodbye and make sure she hasn't changed her mind."

―

"Can you stop by the store before we go home?" Yvette asked.

Jacob gave her a questioning look.

"I want to see if Poppy was right. If the book that I read from had a different cover." She'd been thinking about what Poppy had said, how the book she'd brought Yvette had a broom and magic as part of the illustration while the one at her dad's house didn't. She didn't know why it mattered so much, but for some reason, she couldn't stop thinking about it.

"Sure. It's on the way." Jacob reached over and covered her hand with his. "You were impressive tonight."

Yvette squeezed his fingers, appreciating the words,

but until there was a sign that the curse was broken, she was going to be on pins and needles.

It didn't take long to realize that not only wasn't the curse broken, but things had taken a turn for the worse.

The moment Jacob turned down Main Street, it was obvious that something was terribly off. Earlier in the day, the trouble seemed to be only with the Townsend sisters' family businesses. But now? The entirety of Main Street looked to be cursed.

Most of the gas lamps had burned out, but the few that were still lit were flickering. The one over Incantation Café pulsed, illuminating a crack in the front window.

"Stop here," Yvette told Jacob.

He pulled into a parking spot right in front of the café, and Yvette jumped out to inspect the store, make sure no one had broken in. The door was still locked, but the inside of the shop was dark. The normal fairy lights that kept the store lit after hours were gone. The magical window to the right of the door was dark as well, and the animated spell that had been magically decorating a gingerbread house in a spring theme was gone. The flowers made of frosting that had been in bloom in the small garden in front of the house were now wilted, and the magical fondant butterflies that had been fluttering around the window were now crashed out on the floor. The display was covered in cobwebs, making the springtime scene look more like Halloween had arrived when a spider skittered out of the gingerbread house.

"This is awful. It looks like all the life has been sucked out of Hanna's magic."

"Look," Jacob said, pointing just down the street.

Yvette glanced over at the Mystyk Pizza parlor and let out a small gasp. Lately they'd had their front window spelled to produce a handwritten message specifically for each person who walked by. The last one that Yvette had gotten had complimented her on saying hello to a tourist that had been walking by and then invited her in for a sundried tomato and pesto special at half off. When she politely declined, the message upped the ante by offering her a slice of her favorite cheesecake. It had worked, and she's spent that afternoon walking circles around the bookshop to work off the extra calories.

Today the message was anything but welcoming. In bright neon green it read *Keating Hollow is dead. The magic well has been poisoned.*

As Yvette stared at the warning, the sign began to flash, brighter and then faster and faster and faster until the message finally sizzled out and a puff of smoke appeared, obscuring the window. When it cleared, all that was left was a spiderweb crack all through the glass.

"That was intense," Jacob said.

Yvette looked at her husband and said, "Let's go."

A few minutes later, they were in her store. Yvette

searched high and low for the book that Poppy had brought her the night before, but it was nowhere to be found. Finally she stood in the middle of the store and stretched her arms out.

"Jacob, I need your help," she said.

"Of course," he said, moving closer to her.

"I want to use your air magic to find the book. Take my hand, will you?"

He did as she asked, and once she felt his magic mixing with hers, she guided his air magic to fill the room. She imagined the book flying through the air and right into her other outstretched hand.

Magic tingled from her fingertips and then shot across the room, straight to the children's section of the bookstore. It crawled over all the titles, stopped near the end of the row, and then glowed between two books by authors named Walls and Wunders and then winked out.

Her heart began to race with the implication. The author of the book she was searching for was Maeve Woods. Her magic had gone to the spot where the book had last been placed. Where it should have still been.

"The book isn't here," she whispered. "If it was, our magic would have brought it to me."

"Are we sure the one at your dad's house isn't the same copy?" Jacob asked.

She shrugged. "Poppy said the cover was different. She might be misremembering, but there's no telling in a magical town. It could have shifted once the spell was triggered."

"We need that book, don't we?" he asked.

She nodded grimly. "There's only one thing to do. Get the book and then find Maeve Woods."

## CHAPTER 5

*Y*vette stared at the ceiling, her mind racing as the ache in her gut only intensified. The scene they'd witnessed on Main Street on the way home from her father's house kept replaying on a reel in her mind. Her beloved town was in serious trouble, and sleeping proved to be impossible.

As quietly as she could, Yvette slipped from the bed and shrugged on her robe. She glanced back at her husband, who had somehow managed to fall asleep, and tiptoed out of the room. She headed for the kitchen, made herself a cup of tea, and sat at her desk. After waking up her computer, she typed in *Maeve Woods*.

The author's book came right up, showing the cute cover. Immediately she noted that the version on the internet had a broom and sparkling magic just like Poppy had said. Of all the pictures that showed up online about the book, not one of them had a cover without the broom.

Did her dad somehow have an early edition? Or was the book at her dad's the one from the store that had been magically altered? She had no idea. What she needed to do was find the author.

Maeve Woods didn't have a website, and as far as Yvette could tell, *The Witch of Redwood Grove* was the only title she'd ever published.

Frowning, Yvette clicked on the tab that would only bring up news articles. There were a handful of mostly positive professional reviews and a write up in *The Gazette*, Keating Hollow's local newspaper, but not much else.

She pulled up the article and scanned it. When she got to the last paragraph, she finally found something that might be useful.

*Maeve Woods is the pen name of Marylin Woodsenhoff. She grew up in the redwoods in a small town just outside of Keating Hollow.*

Yvette typed *Marylin Woodsenhoff* along with *address* and came up with absolutely nothing.

Letting out a groan, she deleted the word *address* and did another search. The only information she could find were some posts on a social media site that suggested that Marylin lived in a town called

Moonstone Ridge. The name sounded vaguely familiar, and when she searched maps, she found the tiny unincorporated town was just a few hours away and up the mountain.

"Jackpot," she muttered and wrote the name down on a notepad along with Marylin Woodsenhoff.

A little more searching revealed that Moonstone Ridge was an old mining town that was now considered a ghost town in the Trinity Forest. There was one tiny post office and a gas station, but nothing else other than some old homes and possibly a farm stand.

Yvette was still at her computer trying to search property records for Marylin Woodsenhoff when the sun started to peek in through the window.

"Have you been up all night?" Jacob asked from behind her, startling her.

She jumped in her chair and spun around to find him looking disheveled with dark circles under his eyes. It appeared he hadn't slept well after all. "I got up at three o'clock. Been searching for Maeve Woods."

He placed one hand on her shoulder as he looked down at the notes she'd scribbled on the notepad. "Any luck?"

"A little. Not much. It looks like we're going on a road trip today."

"To Moonstone Ridge?" he asked, raising one eyebrow.

"Yep." She raised her arms and stretched. Her shoulder popped, and she let out a sigh of relief.

"Isn't that the area that gets mudslides every spring?" he asked, frowning.

"Not every spring, but yes, there is a section of the road that seems to get wiped out regularly. The state is trying to reroute the highway, but environmental regulations keep stalling them. For now, there is a bridge that hugs the river that is just wide enough for one car, so traffic can still get in and out."

He nodded. "All right. How about breakfast first, and then we'll swing by your dad's and pick up that book?"

"Sounds good." She glanced at the clock on the wall. It was just after six. "If you'll get breakfast started, I'll go shower the ick off me. I can't shake the feeling that the curse from that book is clinging to me somehow."

"Yvette, that curse is clinging to the entire town. I imagine you could use a flamethrower on your skin and you'd still feel that way."

"That's quite the visual," she said as a small shiver ran down her spine. "Thanks for that."

He chuckled softly. "Sorry. I'll get the bacon on. You go wash off whatever remains of that curse and then fuel up for the day ahead."

Yvette gave him a kiss on the cheek and headed for the shower.

JACOB GLANCED at his wife and said, "Ready?"

She clutched the book she'd just picked up from her father's house and nodded.

He put the Toyota in gear and glanced in the rearview mirror. The kids were on the porch, waving as he and Yvette left the Townsend homestead. Clair was taking the kids to Noel's farm that was right next door so that the cousins could play. If Jacob and Yvette weren't back yet in time for dinner, Clair and Lincoln would take over again.

A pang of regret hit him square in the chest, and he had to fight the urge to turn around and gather their children into his arms and keep them there. But what would he do then? Life in Keating Hollow wouldn't be the same if they didn't figure out how to reverse the curse that Yvette had unknowingly unleashed on them.

He made a left turn out of the Townsend driveway, and when he got to the main highway, instead of going west toward town, he steered the vehicle east toward the mountain and Moonstone Ridge.

"I told my sisters to text me with updates. I want to know if things get worse in the light of day," Yvette said.

Jacob wasn't sure what good that would do. The last thing they needed right now was to be worrying about more issues at home. But he kept his thoughts to himself and said, "Hopefully by the time we roll back into town tonight, all of this will be behind us."

She gave him a skeptical look but said, "From your lips to the goddess's ears."

It wasn't long before they were driving along the river, deep in the redwood forest. The river was gushing with fresh snow melt and was high enough that Jacob imagined one good rainstorm would have them in flood territory.

"I wished for this, you know," Yvette said with a tired sigh.

"For the town to be cursed?" Jacob asked, his eyebrows raised.

"No, of course not." Yvette rolled her eyes at him. "During sisters' night, I wished for us to have more time together. I even envisioned us on a drive through the woods. I saw *this* road. I saw the sun shining through the trees. I never imagined it would be because we were searching for a reclusive author after I ended up cursing the entire town! And I certainly didn't wish for all this anxiety. I swear, if my blood pressure gets any higher, you're gonna have to be on alert for a stroke, because—"

"Yvette," he said, reaching across the vehicle to grab her hand. As he rubbed his thumb over her fingers, doing his best to soothe her, he said, "None of this is your fault."

"But I'm the one—"

"Who read the spell out loud. I know," he said gently. "But you didn't call on your magic. And you certainly weren't cursing anyone. The spell you read aloud was meant to bring peace and harmony, not destruction and despair."

"I know, but in the book, the spell backfires because of bitterness," Yvette argued.

Jacob shook his head as he navigated a curve in the road. "But you're not bitter. Not even close. Of all the people I know, you're the least bitter one out there. You love your job, your kids, your family, and last I checked, you were pretty fond of your husband. What's there to be bitter about?"

That got a small smile out of her. "You're not wrong. I do sort of like my husband." Then she sobered. "What if I'm bitter deep down and no one knows it? I could have harbored some dreams to be a Hollywood movie star or a high-powered businesswoman. What if secretly I'm envious of women who managed to escape their hometowns?"

Jacob let out a huff as he scoffed. "You? Envious? I don't see it. Plus, I think you know that if you did want any of those things, I'd pack the kids up and follow you wherever you wanted to go. So, no. I don't buy it. There is no way you're the reason that spell backfired. It's not your fault that Keating Hollow and your family are mimicking that book. I'm one hundred percent certain that there is something else at play here. Something sinister was cast by someone else, and all of us, including you, are just innocent bystanders who got caught in the fallout."

"One hundred percent?" Yvette asked.

"Yes," he said firmly. "And now, whoever did this is gonna be in a world of hurt, because we both know that no one crosses the Townsend family and gets away with it." He winked at her and reassuringly added, "We'll figure this out, Yvette. And soon enough, the family businesses will be thriving again, and the magic in the store windows will be restored and delighting the tourists just like it does every spring."

"I hope you're right, otherwise..." She stared out the window and finally added, "There is no other alternative."

He squeezed her hand again. "Nothing gets the Townsends down for long. We've got this."

Yvette turned to look at him, her eyes misted with emotion when she said, "I love you, Jacob Burton."

"Good thing, cause I'm not letting you go, Yvette Townsend-Burton. Ever."

"Ever? Now you just sound kinda creepy," she said, laughing softly.

He grinned at her, pleased that he'd been able to pull

her out of her funk. It wasn't often that Yvette got down on herself. And while he understood why she was upset, today was not the day for that. He needed her at the top of her game if they were going to find Maeve Woods and get this curse reversed.

## CHAPTER 6

Yvette knew she'd been a bit of a hot mess as they'd left Keating Hollow. The crushing reality that her beloved town was a mere shell of itself had pained her all the way to her soul. And the very idea that she was the one responsible for the trouble had been tearing her apart.

But then Jacob had been right there to put her back together. To remind her that sometimes awful things happened, but that didn't mean she was the problem. He'd flipped the script to show her that she was privileged enough to be part of the solution, and that was just one of the reasons why she loved him so much. His faith in her and their family was unwavering.

It was the exact message she needed to hear to get her head on straight.

They had a job to do, and dammit, she was going to do it. One way or another, she'd find a way to fix it.

"I think we're getting close," she said as they passed a summit sign. "I'm pretty sure the tiny post office is just around the bend."

"Got it," Jacob said. "I saw a couple houses back there, tucked behind the river, so that makes sense."

Yvette had noticed the houses, too. Both looked like summer cabins, though neither had shown any signs of life yet. "There!" Yvette pointed to the right. "Turn here."

Jacob made a quick right turn and then slowed as they followed the road underneath the highway away from the river and into what must have been the town of Moonstone Ridge.

"Town" had been overstating things. Moonstone Ridge had a gas station with one fuel pump and a small convenience store attached. Yvette was willing to guess that if one was hungry, their options were stale chips, soda, and candy bars. The only other building in downtown Moonstone Ridge was a small white storefront that had the US Flag flying out front.

"That must be the post office," Yvette said, pointing at it.

Jacob pulled the SUV into the deserted parking lot and killed the engine.

Yvette hopped out and waited impatiently for Jacob to

join her. When he hit the button to lock the doors of their Sequoia, she smirked at him. "Who do you think is going to steal it? A random deer who happens to walk by?"

He snorted and then shrugged. "Habit." He held his hand out to her, and when she took it, he said, "Let's go find out where Marylin Woodsenhoff lives."

"I thought you'd never ask," she muttered.

"I heard that," he shot back, but Yvette ignored him as she stepped through the door to the post office.

The building smelled of musky dampness, and the floor looked like it hadn't been swept in forever. A florescent light flickered above, making her eye twitch. "Hello?" she called out.

The word echoed through the place.

"Looks deserted," Jacob said.

"If that were true, the light wouldn't even be on," Yvette said, leaning forward at the front counter and trying to see if she could peer into the back room. There was grime around the edges of everything, but the counter and the floor directly behind it seemed to have been cleaned recently as neither were covered in dust. Then she spotted a full mail bag just behind the counter. "Someone is here. We just need to find them."

"Maybe they're in the restroom," he said as he walked away from the counter and moved toward the wall of post office boxes.

"Who are you?" a raspy voice asked from behind Yvette.

She straightened and spun to find a wrinkled older woman with white hair and watery blue eyes staring at her. "I'm Yvette Townsend-Burton, and that's my husband, Jacob."

"Good for you," the woman said, looking disinterested as she slipped behind the counter.

*What did that mean?* Good for you? Hadn't she just asked Yvette who she was?

Yvette cleared her throat. "We're looking for someone named Marylin Woodsenhoff. Can you—"

The woman straightened, adding nearly two inches to her overall height. She stared Yvette down when she said, "If you know what's good for you, forget about that name. Get in that fancy vehicle out there and drive out of this town right now. And don't ever look back."

"But—"

"Don't ever look back!" she cried as she disappeared into the back room.

Yvette turned to find Jacob standing right behind her. "Now what?"

Jacob eyed the doorway she'd disappeared through, and then after what appeared to be some sort of internal debate, he shrugged and slipped behind the counter. A second later, he followed the strange woman into the back room.

Unable to stand the suspense, Yvette hurried after him. But as soon as she crossed the threshold into the room, she came to a complete stop. Jacob was completely alone in a small space that couldn't have been more than eight feet square, and there didn't appear to be any other doors or windows. "Where did she go?"

He shook his head. "Unless there's a trap door, she must have figured out how to teleport, because I don't see another exit."

"She didn't teleport," Yvette said, frustrated. "I'm sure there's a secret door here somewhere." She started to run her hands around the chipped molding but stopped the moment she came into contact with a spider. She let out a cry that sounded more like a scream before taking a step back and deciding that she just didn't care about a secret passage anymore.

"Come on," Jacob said, leading her back up front. "We're not going to find anything here. Maybe someone at the gas station will have some information."

"Wait," Yvette said as she eyed the bag of mail that was still sitting behind the counter. "I think we have everything we need already."

"What—" Jacob started.

Yvette grinned up at him as she grabbed a handful of letters from the bag and started to scan the names. The mail bag was mostly full of advertisements, but there were a few personal letters and utility bills as well.

"You know that tampering with mail is against the law, right?" Jacob asked.

"I'm not tampering," she said. "I'm browsing."

"If you say so."

"Come on, Jacob. Help me. The sooner we find her address, the sooner we can get out of this mold-infested building."

"When you put it that way," he said and reached into the bag to grab some mail.

They spent the next ten minutes going through an impressive amount of junk mail that was mostly addressed to *Current Resident*. Yvette was ready to throw in the towel and try the gas station across the street when Jacob finally let out a whoop of excitement.

"Got it!" He held out an envelope that was addressed to Marylin Woodsenhoff.

"Oh my gosh! You're my knight in shining armor." Yvette threw her arms around him, giving him a giant hug. Then she took out her phone, snapped a picture of the address, and dropped the letter back into the mailbag. "See? No tampering whatsoever."

"You're the very picture of a model citizen," he teased.

"Let's get out of here," she said and grabbed his hand, tugging him behind her. Just as they exited the building, Yvette heard the voice of the unfriendly woman from earlier.

"Turn around and never come back!" The woman's raspy voice grated on Yvette's nerves.

"Did you hear that?" she asked Jacob as she glanced around, looking for the older lady.

"Hear what?"

"The old mail lady. The one who went into the back room but never came out," Yvette said. "She told us to turn around and never come back."

"Nope," Jacob said. "Doesn't matter now anyway. We have to find Ms. Marylin, and now we have an address. We're not leaving now."

Yvette grinned at him. "This is why you're my ride or die person. You know that, right?"

"I'm your ride or die for other, dirtier reasons, but I'll take that for now." He opened the SUV's passenger door for her and flashed a lascivious wink.

Yvette stared at him for a beat and then smirked before climbing in. She quickly mapped the address and was ready to go when Jacob looked at her expectantly. "Get back on the highway going east. In ten miles, we exit and head up the mountain."

"Leave it to a witch to live in the middle of nowhere," he said and then put the vehicle in gear.

## CHAPTER 7

The SUV rattled and shook as Jacob drove over the uneven gravel road that likely hadn't been graded in years. He swerved, trying to miss one hole, but promptly landed in another one, sending them both bouncing high enough that Jacob's head hit the roof of the SUV. He let out a groan and leaned forward, trying his best to see any hazards in the shade from the redwoods.

"I think we're almost there," Yvette said. She was squinting at her mapping software, but it had already failed them twice and they'd ended up at two dead ends before turning around to try again.

"If we don't get there soon, I'm afraid we might lose the suspension," Jacob muttered as he gritted his teeth and jerked to avoid yet another pothole.

"Good thing you're an air witch," Yvette said. "You'd be able to repair it at least long enough to get us home."

He glanced at her, took in her smug expression, and then went back to concentrating on the road. She was right, of course. If a tire blew or the suspension was shot, his magic would be enough for at least a temporary fix. The realization eased some of his tension, making it easier to navigate.

The road suddenly came to a dead end, and Jacob let out a curse. "Dammit. We're never going to find this place."

"We have to," Yvette said calmly and then got out of the vehicle.

Jacob ran his hands through his hair and then joined her.

"Do you feel that?" she asked as she raised her hand.

"All I feel is a slight breeze," he said, frustrated and more than a little impatient.

"Exactly. It's just enough to cast a finding spell." She smiled up at him. "I can help you if you want."

A finding spell. Why hadn't he thought of that? Jacob was an air witch. If he cast a finding spell, the air would guide him to help him find Marylin, and it certainly would be more accurate than Yvette's phone app had been. "Let's do it."

"I need a piece of paper," Yvette said as she yanked the SUV's door open again. "And a pen."

"Check the console." Jacob stood facing the mountain, just knowing that they were close to Marylin's house. He could feel it. He just couldn't see it.

"Got them both." Yvette returned and held out a tiny slip of paper to him. "Take this. Put it in the palm of your hand and make a fist. Hold on until I tell you to let go."

Jacob did as he was told. While he had air magic, he wasn't exactly an expert at casting spells. It just wasn't something he ran around doing all the time.

Yvette took his free hand and said, "Now imagine the written address in your hand floating on the wind. Imagine it floating right toward Marylin's house."

"I don't know what it looks like," he said.

"Just imagine any old house. Or a cabin if you prefer. The details don't matter here. It's the intention."

"Okay. I've got it." He imagined a gorgeous log cabin with smoke wafting from the chimney. There was a horse right outside, along with two goats.

"Good. Now repeat after me," Yvette said. "Goddess of light, use my knowledge and my air magic to help me track down Ms. Marylin Woodsenhoff."

He repeated it. The wind picked up instantly.

"Release the paper now," Yvette ordered.

Jacob did as he was told, and immediately the paper turned into what look like a ball of fairy light.

"Perfect." Yvette ran back to the SUV. "Get in. We have to follow it!"

"On it." Jacob jumped back into the vehicle and was grateful when the fairy light didn't take off like a rocket. It wasn't exactly slow, but it wasn't a speed demon either, and that alone probably saved him from blowing all four tires.

They wove back through the gravel road, following the light until it came to a stop in the middle of a pretty lavender-covered meadow.

Jacob glanced around and frowned. "It doesn't look like our spell worked."

Yvette grinned. "Yes it did. Look."

He followed her gaze and spotted a pale stream of smoke that seemed to appear out of nowhere in the exact place where a chimney might be. Jacob killed the motor and climbed out of the SUV. The second his feet hit the ground, the lavender field faded away and was replaced with a patchy grass field that looked like it hadn't been mowed or maintained anytime recently.

"Look," Yvette whispered as she pointed off to the left. "The house is over there."

He followed her gaze. When he didn't see anything, he blinked, and suddenly a large two-story Victorian house appeared out of nowhere. It had a large wraparound porch and gingerbread trim. In its heyday, it must have been gorgeous. But now it suffered from peeling paint and rotted siding. Weeds grew up against the porch, and at least two of the windows were broken.

The front door swung open with a loud screech, and a gorgeous woman with long strawberry-blond hair walked out onto the porch. She wore a white peasant blouse, rolled up jeans, and a straw hat. She fixed her gaze on them and said, "You're trespassing."

"Marylin Woodsenhoff?" Yvette called. "Are you Maeve Woods?"

The woman on the porch jerked back as if someone had slapped her, but she quickly recovered and again said, "You're trespassing. Get in that giant vehicle and go home. Now."

"We can't," Yvette said, holding up her hands as if she were being threatened and she wanted to surrender. "We have to ask you about your book, *The Witch of Redwood Grove*."

"I'm warning you now," the woman spat out. "Leave now or else suffer the consequences."

"But—" Yvette was suddenly silenced, and with a flick of her finger, the witch standing on the porch forced Jacob's wife to march herself into an enclosed overgrown garden. The latch closed with a loud clicking noise that rang in Jacob's ears.

"What did you do to her?" he demanded, racing for the garden. But he'd barely taken a few steps when he was stopped by sticky magic, and before he knew what was happening, his feet were carrying him toward the woman on the porch. He tried to slow down or command his feet to stop moving, but it was no use. He was under her spell and there was nothing he could do.

"You should have left when you had the chance," she said when he came to a stop in front of her. At this range, Jacob could see that the witch wasn't that gorgeous after all. From afar, she looked soft and rosy and full of life. But up close, he couldn't help but notice the crow's-feet affecting both eyes and her sun-spotted skin.

The woman, while still pretty, was showing her age. If he had to guess, he'd say mid to late sixties. But honestly, these days, how could anyone know?

"Release my wife," Jacob ordered her.

"When I'm ready," she said. "Until then, you and I are going to have a talk." She crooked her finger, and once again Jacob seemed to be under her spell. He followed her into the dust-filled home and tried not to wheeze.

"This way."

The floors creaked under their feet, and Jacob started to wonder if he was going to fall right through the wooden slats.

Another door flew open. There was no light, and quickly he realized that there was a stairwell that likely led to a basement. "Is this where you throw me into the basement and then chop up my limbs for your freezer?" he asked.

Her gaze ran up and down the length of his body as if she were contemplating that very thing. But then she gave him an evil smile and said, "There will be no cutting of limbs. I have other uses for you." Then she shoved him, sending him flying down the stairs into a dark pit of the unknown.

He let out a cry of alarm as his shoulder hit what he assumed to be the stairs. His body bounced painfully as he slid the rest of the way until he landed with a soft thud on what felt like some sort of area rug. Jacob carefully tested his limbs to make sure nothing was broken. When he was certain he was going to live, he rolled over onto his back and let out a groan as he felt every one of his aches and pains.

An overhead light came on and Marylin was standing over him, evaluating the situation. "Do you like your accommodations?"

Jacob blinked at her and then looked around, finding a large bed that was made up with over a dozen pillows and a fluffy down comforter that he guessed would feel like sleeping on a cloud. There were ornate antique floor lamps, a grandfather clock, and a vintage settee that was set up in the sitting area. This room had been meticulously decorated and cared for, unlike the outside of the house. "This is… nice," he said. "It would be nicer if my wife were here instead of locked up outside in an overgrown garden."

Marylin walked up to him, ran her fingernail over his lips, and then let it trail down his chin to the opening of his shirt. She leaned in close and whispered, "But I don't share."

He ground his teeth together. "I'm a married man who isn't interested in cheating on his wife."

"I didn't ask what you were interested in, did I, Mr...."

"Burton," he supplied. He saw no reason to withhold information. All he wanted was to make sure that Yvette was okay.

"Nice." Marylin licked her lips and said, "Now, you and me, we're going to get to know each other really well. Then we'll talk about your wife."

"No," he said again and moved away from her. It was strange that he didn't seem to be under her spell anymore. Ever since she'd shoved him into the room, he'd had free will. And he'd definitely use it if she kept up her advances. But instead of playing her game, he blurted out, "We're here about your children's book. Two days ago, a curse was unleashed from it, and we need your help to reverse it."

Her eyes went from a vibrant green to almost pure black when she said, "That's impossible. I destroyed every copy of that book after I learned it was cursed."

"Well, one seems to have escaped you," Jacob said. "In fact, it's in the SUV right now."

Marylin froze for a long moment, and then without another word, she flew up the stairs. The door slammed and the echo reverberated through the entire house.

Jacob raced up the stairs and yanked on the door. The force sent him flying back to the floor, but the door didn't move.

He tried again. While the knob turned, the door wouldn't budge, and Jacob felt a slight trace of magic. It was spelled shut.

He scanned the room for windows, and when he didn't see any, that's when he started to panic. With his air magic, windows were always a surefire way to escape any room. But now? He needed to figure out how to reverse her spell or put some holes in the walls.

Reversing a spell he didn't know anything about was a reach. And holes were going to be impossible considering the walls appeared to be made of concrete.

Frustrated, he tugged at the ends of his hair and started to pace the room, ignoring the backache and the twinge in his left knee. There had to be a way out. Something he hadn't thought of yet. He passed a large armoire, and that's when he saw it. Black curtains hung over a small opening.

He ran to the wall, ripped the curtains open, and pumped his fist when he saw the small access window.

Jacob wasted no time gathering his magic. *Hold on, Yvette*, he thought. *I'm coming.*

## CHAPTER 8

Yvette was so angry she could have spit nails. The overgrown garden was full of prickly weeds with exactly one live plant right in the middle. She stared at the tall sunflower and cursed its cheerful nature. It was like a slap in the face considering that she could feel magic was binding her to the earth. She was able to go right up to the wooden enclosure that surrounded the garden, but the moment she tried to grab on and climb out, the posts grew spikes that protruded from the boards, making it impossible for her to climb without tearing up her hands and bare skin.

The sun was beating down on her, and sweat started to sting her eyes. She had to find a way out of this magical enclosure and into that house where Marylin had taken her husband. She took a few steps back, cursed when a weed started to wind its way around her ankle, and then jerked back, ripping the weed from the soil. It instantly died, drying up into a brittle brown remnant of itself.

More vine-like weeds came for her, and suddenly she found herself yanking weed after weed from the soil, trying to keep from becoming tied up like a mummy or buried in the overgrowth. Horror filled her as she wondered just how many people Marylin had fed to the garden over the years. Had people come looking for her and then just completely disappeared?

The thought had her redoubling her efforts to pull more and more weeds until she found herself standing in a cleared area, breathing hard and sweating right through her T-shirt.

"Well, isn't this a nice perk," Marylin said from outside the garden enclosure, sounding pleased. "It's been ages since the garden has looked that good. Maybe if you get it weeded entirely, I'll let you clean the house next."

"Let me out of here," Yvette demanded.

"Why would I do that?" The witch looked completely perplexed.

"Because if you don't, you're not going to like what happens next."

Marylin threw her head back and laughed. "You're feisty. I like that. Just like your husband. You two are going to be fun to have around."

Yvette curled her hands into fists and felt her magic simmering just beneath the surface. "Where is Jacob?"

"Oh, he's comfortable inside. No doubt waiting impatiently for me to get back to what we started." Marylin's smile didn't reach her eyes, making her look more like an evil demon than a witch. Considering the fact that she'd written a children's book that actually cursed people, Yvette was definitely leaning toward soulless demon.

"What do you want from us?" Yvette tried, hoping that if she could get the woman talking she'd get some answers.

"Isn't it obvious?" Marylin asked, tilting her head to the side as she studied Yvette.

"No. Not unless making us miserable is all you're interested in."

She shrugged. "That would be enough on its own, I suppose. Why should I be the only one who's had to suffer? But that's not what I want."

Questions raced through Yvette's mind. What had happened to this witch, and why was she so bitter? And what was her next move? Yvette softened her tone when she asked, "You suffered?"

Marylin let out a loud bark of laughter. "Isn't it obvious?" She flung an arm out, waving around at her property. "At one time this was a glorious house with lovely gardens, and it was full of family. Now look at it.

Look at me! Everything here is dying. But now you and your handsome husband are here. With him by my side and you cleaning things up, we could restore this place to its former glory. Can't you see it? Me and Jacob, right there on a freshly painted porch, sipping lemonade as our kids play in the lavender fields."

Yvette stared at her with her jaw hanging open. Was the woman insane? She thought she might be. "Jacob isn't going to stay here with you, Marylin. And if you think I'm going to be some sort of servant, you've clearly lost the last of your marbles. We're here to reverse a curse, not step into your delusional fantasy."

"I'm the one with the power here!" the woman cried ominously. Lightning flashed through the bright blue sky as if to prove her point. "You'll do what I say. Or else—"

"Or else what? You'll let your destructive garden eat me?" Yvette spat back.

"That's exactly what I'll do." She waved a hand toward the garden enclosure, and suddenly all the weeds were back. They wrapped around both her arms and legs, binding Yvette to the spot where she stood.

Adrenaline took over, and suddenly fire poured from Yvette's palms. She pointed her hands toward the ground, quickly burning the weeds back. As soon as her arms were free, she burned a wide circle around herself, causing the weeds to retreat quickly.

"Cute trick," Marylin said dryly. "Fire witches are such a pain in my ass."

"She's not the only one who's going to be a pain in your ass!" Jacob shouted as he held his arms out and send what looked like a gale force of wind directly at her.

Marylin was swept off her feet and thrown forcibly into the garden fence. She let out an anguished cry as she hit one of the beams and then crumpled to the ground in front of him. She looked up at him with tears in her eyes. "Why did you do that?"

"Why?" he raged at her. "Why? You locked me in your sex basement and confined my wife in a torture garden. I'd think it's obvious."

She blinked up at him, looking confused.

Yvette snapped. "Drop the act, Marylin! You're not fooling anyone. Let me out of here right now, or I'll burn this place down. Understand?"

"I—I can't," she stuttered. "It's not me. I—" Her face morphed into something truly terrifying as she spat out, "Shut up, you imbecile. Remember what happened the last time you defied me?"

"What?" Yvette asked.

"I didn't do anything," Marylin said in a higher-pitched tone, sounding both scared and a little angry. "It's not my fault—" Her lips clamped shut as Marylin shook her head. Her eyes morphed from pale green to deep blue, and her features changed from those of the gorgeous strawberry blonde they'd first seen on the porch to a woman with wider-set eyes and unruly curly black hair. She would have been striking if it weren't for the pure hatred that was pouring out of her. "Everything is your fault. It always has been. If it weren't for me, you'd be in prison right now after that curse you cast."

The woman morphed once again to the strawberry blonde, and this time there was fury radiating off her. "I did not cast that curse. You did! You ruined my life, and now here you are again, ruining this couple's life because of your greed and jealousy!"

"Shut up!" Marylin stood, all traces of the strawberry-blond woman gone, replaced by the fiery dark-haired witch with the Medusa curls. She wore black combat boots, black leggings, a gray skirt, and a ripped black T-shirt. She could have appeared right out of an eighties grunge video. Then she turned on Jacob and crooked her finger at him. "You, come here."

Jacob took a jerky step forward, his face red and his hands fisted.

"Not on my watch!" Yvette cried as she unleashed her fire magic. It burst from her hands and lit the post in front of her, instantly setting the dried wood aflame. Smoke billowed up, blinding her momentarily until she could direct the smoke away from her to clear the air.

As soon as the smoke dissipated, Yvette scanned the

area for her husband but couldn't find him anywhere. "Jacob!" she called.

The only sound was the crackling of the fire she'd started.

She stood in that forsaken garden, nearly going out of her mind as she waited for the fire to do its job.

What had she just witnessed? The only possible explanation was that two women were sharing one body. It was likely that the dark-haired witch had taken over Marylin's body and was controlling her. But who was the dark-haired witch, how had she ended up in Marylin's body, and which one of them was responsible for the curse? Was Marylin actually innocent and had been being tortured all these years?

There were no answers at hand.

Not until she could find Marylin.

Yvette paced in front of the fire, adding more flames, but no matter what she did, the wood wouldn't turn to ash. It just burned and burned and burned, leaving her trapped in hell.

She spun around and then froze when she saw the sunflower staring right at her. Or more accurately, she saw Marylin's face staring at her from the center of the sunflower. The strawberry-blond version with the pale green eyes.

"Marylin?" Yvette asked tentatively.

The sunflower nodded and then spoke. "My sister is

more powerful than I am. The vines, those are her creation. This sunflower is my contribution to the garden. It irritates her to no end that her weeds can't kill it."

Yvette blinked at the sunflower, wondering if she'd lost her mind.

"She has control of my body now," Marylin said. "That could only mean one thing."

When the sunflower didn't elaborate, Yvette said, "And what's that?"

"The curse has been activated."

Dread crawled up Yvette's throat, nearly choking her. "What curse is that?"

"The one that was meant to destroy me. Find the broom, and you can end the curse." The face in the middle of the sunflower vanished, and suddenly two more plants popped up from the ground and grew rapidly until there were three sunflowers tilting their petals toward the sun.

"Find the broom?! What does that mean?" Yvette cried. But then the image of the children's book flashed in her mind. Was she talking about the broom on the cover? The one that Poppy said was there and then wasn't? The one that was in the online photos but not on the book that had shown up at her father's house? That had to be it. She turned back to the sunflowers and desperately asked, "Where would I even look for that broom?"

The three sunflowers were silent as they continued to soak up the sun.

"Well, it's not in this desecrated garden," she muttered. "First thing's first. I've got to get out of here." The fire she'd started earlier was still lit, but it wasn't burning anything, making it useless. She walked over and imagined that the fire was extinguished, causing the flames to suddenly disappear. Just as she'd suspected, the only burn marks that existed were the ones on the ground. The weeds had been burned back, leaving a small gap between the wooden structure and the ground.

Yvette crouched down and dug at the dirt, finding that the burned surface was easy to move away from the fence. She slid her hand under the wooden frame of the garden enclosure, checking to make sure no magical barrier below it was keeping her in place, and then got to work on digging herself out.

## CHAPTER 9

"You'll never get what you want from me," Jacob said with a sneer as he stared at the black-haired witch. Her magic had been intense when she'd marched him back into the basement, and the air was so thick with it that he'd almost been unable to breathe. It was a little better now, but every time he tried to reach for his own air magic, it just left him out of breath.

She tossed her head back and laughed. "You have no idea what I want."

Jacob glanced down at the magical bindings that were holding him to the bed and raised one eyebrow. "You're hardly a witch of mystery."

"Well, that. Sure. Do you know how long it's been since I've been with a man? In this body, I mean? *Years.*

And you're young and handsome. You should take it as a compliment that I'm even considering letting you seduce me."

He snorted. "Seduce? I don't even know your name."

She gave him a curious look. "Does that really matter to men?"

Wow. This woman was a piece of work. "I'm going to go out on a limb and say that yes, it does."

"Fine. It's Kariann. Better?"

At least he knew her name, but that wouldn't change anything. He'd let her touch him over his dead body. "What's your relationship to Marylin?" he asked, hoping to distract her.

"I don't want to talk about my sister right now. She's taken enough from me already." Kariann moved to sit next to Jacob, placing her hand on his thigh.

He twitched, trying to get away from her. His skin crawled as his mind raced, trying to come up with a plan to get out of his current predicament. If he couldn't wield his air magic, his only choice was pure blunt force. He'd have to get her to untie him first though.

"Now don't be like that. I don't bite." She pumped her eyebrows. "Unless you want me to."

He swallowed the bile that rose to the back of his throat. "What I want is for you to untie me. I'm not into bondage."

She gave him a flat stare. "Do you think I'm an idiot?"

"Do you think I'm a whore?"

Kariann's lips quirked into an amused smile.

He wanted to wipe that look right off her face, but he schooled his features and asked, "What else do you want, besides... this?"

"Isn't it obvious? I want to be free of Marylin's body and this depressing farmhouse. I want to be free to live however I want without her always judging me. All I need is more power. If I take you, I'll have enough power to finally break the ties that have bound us together for the last eight months."

"You think having sex with me will give you the power to break free from your sister?" he asked, feeling fairly scandalized.

She let out a bark of humorless laughter. "Sex? Now that's funny. There's no time for that right now, handsome. Though, if you survive when this is all over, we can revisit the idea then."

He blinked at her, confused. "I thought..." He shook his head. "What's all this about then? Why do you have me tied to the bed, and why is your hand still on my thigh?"

"You're a handsome man. A girl can fantasize, can't she?"

He was tired of her games. "Just tell me what you want."

"Your magic, of course." Her tone was light and airy as

if she hadn't just told him her plan was to steal something as vital to him as his very soul.

"I don't think so," he said, glaring at her.

"You don't have a choice." Kariann moved in and covered his mouth with hers.

Jacob jerked his head away from her, but she just crawled on top of him and forced him down onto his back, all while keeping her mouth locked with his. He jerked his head from side to side, but her hands came up, holding him in a vice-like grip, determined to take what wasn't hers. He kicked and bucked and then finally settled as he tried to focus on the magic that she'd latched on to and was successfully sucking from his body.

He imagined his magic concentrating at his palms, and suddenly instead of it pouring into her it was rushing down his arms and into his hands. He couldn't manipulate it in any way. Couldn't unleash it to remove his bindings or to force Kariann off him, but at least he'd stopped her from stealing his magic.

It was a start.

Kariann redoubled her efforts, squeezing his head so tightly that he felt as if it might explode. His entire body was coiled with tension as he did everything he could to keep control of his magic. All of his muscles started to ache, and his head pounded. He wasn't sure how much longer he could hold out.

And then, suddenly Jacob felt heat burning his wrists.

He jerked and the restraints ripped away. Immediately, he grabbed Kariann's wrists and forced her hands away from his head. Once he was free from her grip, he grabbed her by the arms and forcefully removed her from his body.

"No one seduces my husband," Yvette said right before she swung one of the floor lamps and clobbered Kariann in the head with the base. The witch slumped over and then crumpled onto the floor of the basement.

"Yvette," Jacob cried as he jumped up from the bed, all the magic that had been restraining him gone. "Are you all right?"

"Are you?" She grabbed his arms and inspected his wrists. "I'm sorry I burned you. I didn't know what else to do. She had her lips locked to yours, and I was afraid if I attacked her I'd hit you. The way she was smothering you with her lips, I couldn't be sure I wouldn't miss and hit you both."

"What?" He glanced down at his wrists, and when he saw his singed skin, he understood what had happened. Yvette had gotten into the basement and had used her fire magic to burn away his restraints. "It's all right. When we get home, I'll go to the healer. I'm sure they'll get me fixed up."

Yvette lurched forward and wrapped her arms around Jacob, holding on tightly. "I'm sorry I didn't get here sooner."

He clutched her. "I'm sorry you were left outside. How did you get in here?"

She pulled back and then held her hands up. They were covered in dirt and so were her T-shirt and jeans.

"Did you dig your way out of the garden?" he asked, gently inspecting her hands. A couple of her fingers were raw and red with blood.

"I did what I had to. What exactly was going on in here? I saw that wench forcing herself on you. Is that really what she wanted? Any man to..." She waved her hand in the air. "To *satisfy* her?"

He couldn't help the inappropriate laughter that bubbled up from the back of his throat.

"It's not funny, Jacob," she said, looking over at the witch who was still sprawled out on the floor.

"Sorry. She didn't want that. She wanted my magic," he said quickly. "She was going to suck it right out of me."

Yvette's eyes got wide and then she snarled as she looked at the witch on the ground. "That miserable old crow. She was going to *steal* your magic?"

He nodded as he stood and looked at her. "She's sharing a body with her sister and wants to be free. She thinks more power will help her achieve that goal."

"That's... insane. Would she take your body, too?"

"I'm guessing she planned to take Marylin's. Kill her off and keep her shell, maybe."

Yvette closed her eyes and grimaced. "What do we do now? We can't just leave."

"We still need to figure out how to reverse the curse in Keating Hollow," Jacob said. "You haven't forgotten why we came here, have you?"

"Oh, right. Marylin told me that we need to find the missing broom. I think she meant the one that should be on the cover. She said then we could reverse the curse."

"How?" Jacob asked.

"She disappeared before she could elaborate. All I know is that our next mission is to find that broom."

"A finding spell?" he asked.

"I think so. Between the two of us, I think we can do it." Yvette looked at Kariann. "What do we do about her?"

"We can't leave her here like this. She's too dangerous. We better take her to Drew," he said, already kneeling beside the woman. "What should we bind her with?"

Yvette picked up a pair of pink furry handcuffs, holding them with just her thumb and forefinger. "Will these do?"

He groaned but then nodded. "It's probably the best we've got. I'll reinforce them with my air magic."

"Better use this too." She handed him a silk scarf. "Use it as a gag. We can't have her muttering spells if she comes to on the way back to town."

He nodded and got to work.

## CHAPTER 10

Yvette followed Jacob as he hauled Kariann out of the house and into the SUV. He placed her in the back seat and then slammed the door.

"I hate that she's in the Sequoia," he said, scowling at the door.

"Me, too, but what else can we do?" Yvette said as color from the garden caught her eye. She walked a few feet over to get a better look and saw that there were now five tall sunflowers, all with their faces tilted to the sun.

"Does the house look... *better* than it did when we first got here?" Jacob asked.

"What do you mean by *better*?" she asked, but as soon as she focused on the house, she knew exactly what he meant. The paint, while still faded, wasn't peeling, and she could no longer see any dry rot. One of the windows that she'd have sworn was broken was now a solid piece of glass that gleamed in the sunlight. "Is it healing itself?"

"Maybe?"

"The garden is trying, too," she said, turning around to look at the sunflowers once more. "The weeds are dying off on their own, and the sunflowers seem to be taking over. Marylin told me that the weeds are her sister's contribution. Marylin planted the sunflowers."

"Do you think expelling Kariann from the house will return it to its former glory?" Jacob asked.

"I hope so." But Yvette had more important things to worry about. "Let's do that finding spell. If the broom is here, we don't want to leave without finding it."

Yvette grabbed the first aid kit and a small bag of supplies from the back of the SUV. After cleaning her own hands, she applied antiseptic ointment to her scrapes and then to Jacob's wrists, covering them both with clean bandages. Then she grabbed the spellcasting supplies and motioned for Jacob to follow her to a clearing away from the house and the garden.

They both got to work creating the pentagram and salt circle. Once that was done, Yvette took the lead at the northern most point while Jacob stood across from her.

"Ready?" she asked.

"Ready."

They both raised their arms in the air. The wind

immediately picked up, swirling around them while a fire came to life right in the middle of the pentagram.

"Goddess of the earth," Yvette called. "We seek knowledge. Wind and fire, fire and wind, combine our magic and give us the sight. Reveal the broom we seek. Fire and wind, wind and fire, reveal the broom. Help us reverse another witch's ire!"

The wind whipped around them as the fire grew, forming a massive ball in the pentagram, obscuring Jacob from Yvette's view. She stared into the flames, mesmerized by the force of it until suddenly the wind stopped and a scene formed in the fireball.

Yvette let out a gasp and cried, "It's back at the bookstore!"

The fireball instantly disappeared, leaving Yvette and Jacob staring at each other.

"Can that be right?" Jacob asked. "The broom is at the shop?"

She shrugged. "The book was there at one time. I suppose it's possible the broom is there now. All I know is that I saw an ornate hand-carved broom that I don't recognize in the corner of the stockroom, hidden behind a bookcase."

Jacob held out his hand to her. "Then we better go."

After checking on Kariann and finding her awake but still fully restrained, Yvette climbed into the passenger seat and took one last look at the Victorian home.

Flowers had popped up around the border of the porch, and the field off to the right had a couple of bushes of lavender that were blooming.

Yvette turned around in her seat and met Kariann's gaze. "Looks like the place is happy to see you go."

Kariann jerked and squirmed, obviously trying to loosen her restraints. When it didn't work, she just glared at Yvette. Yvette glared back.

Jacob hopped into the SUV and took off back down the gravel road without a word. It didn't take long to realize that there weren't nearly as many potholes on the way out as there had been on the way in.

Yvette shook her head at Kariann. "It appears your brand of poison had a long reach."

Kariann let out a grunt and then stared out the window.

Yvette settled back into her seat, wishing there was a way to teleport back to Keating Hollow. It had already been a long day.

~

"It doesn't look like anything has changed," Yvette said with a heavy heart when they finally made the turn onto Main Street. The gas lamps were all out, and weeds had popped up between the cobblestones on the sidewalks.

All of the businesses were shuttered except for a few of the restaurants, and even those looked like a ghost town.

When they'd driven through Moonstone Ridge, the post office building had looked freshly painted, and to her surprise, there were half a dozen cars at the gas station. The drivers were buying snacks and waiting their turn to fill up at the single gas pump. Yvette had hoped that meant Keating Hollow was healing, too, but no such luck.

Jacob reached across the console and squeezed her hand. "I'm sure once we reverse the curse, everything will go back to normal." He glanced in the rearview mirror briefly before turning his attention back to the road as he pulled into the parking lot of the sheriff's department.

They'd called to warn Drew Baker they were coming as soon as they got to a spot with a cell signal, and he walked out of the building just as they parked. He wasted no time opening the back door and hauling Kariann out of the vehicle.

"Thanks, Drew," Yvette said. "Be careful with her. She's powerful. As near as we can tell, she's harboring two magical souls. So up the security or you might find one of them trying to escape."

Drew sucked in a sharp breath. "The Magical Task Force is already on the way, but I'll personally keep a close eye on her until they get here."

"Good plan," Jacob said, clapping his brother-in-law on the back.

"What's this?" Drew asked as he looked at the pink handcuffs.

Yvette felt her face flush with heat and said, "We made do with what we could find. You probably want to put some real magical cuffs on her, but I wouldn't remove the gag until the MTF gets here. She's... not super pleasant."

Drew chuckled. "Pink fuzzy handcuffs. Now I've seen it all."

"I'm glad you're amused," Jacob said. "You might be singing a different story if she'd been trying to use them on you."

"Pardon?" Drew asked.

"I'll tell you later," Jacob said. "Right now, we're going to see if we can figure out how to reverse this curse that's ruining Keating Hollow. We'll be back to make our statements."

Yvette clung to Jacob's hand, itching to get to the bookstore.

Without any traffic and no tourists, it didn't take long to get to Hollow Books. Yvette grabbed the book and jumped out of the car. She was so anxious to get inside that her hands were shaking as she tried to unlock the door.

Jacob gently took the key from her and then calmly opened the door.

Yvette stepped into her store and wrinkled her nose when she caught a whiff of stale, musty air. Normally when she walked in, she was greeted with the lovely scent of bound leather and coffee. It had turned into her favorite scent combination because it represented one of her favorite places on earth. But now, all she could smell was dampness and mildew. It made her stomach churn.

She hated what the curse had done to her shop, her family, her town. And no matter what she and Jacob had been through, it was worth it to bring back everything they loved.

Yvette took off for the stockroom. She tore through the door and ran for the bookcase that she'd seen in the fire. But when she got there, the broom was nowhere to be found.

"What?" she cried out. "I saw it here. Right here." She pointed to the spot near the bookcase. "Right, Jacob? That's where it's supposed to be, isn't it?"

He nodded, his expression grim.

Yvette spun back around, searching everywhere for the broom. Had Brinn been there today? She didn't think so, but she picked up the nearby phone and dialed anyway.

It went straight to voice mail.

"Dammit." She left the stockroom and went into her office. After practically tearing it apart, she then scoured the bookshop sales floor, looking anywhere and everywhere for the broom.

Nothing.

"It's not over here either," Jacob called from the coffee shop area.

"It has to be here somewhere!" she cried as she went back into the stockroom, walked up to the bookcase, and started to move it. Just as she nudged it to the left, she heard something clatter to the ground. But as she scanned the old wood floor, she didn't see anything.

Certain that she was losing her mind, she dropped to her knees and started to run her hands over the wood. Almost immediately, her hand wrapped around something hard and grooved. As she tightened her grip, the broom revealed itself.

"Son of a monkey," she said under her breath. "It's been here the entire time?"

"Yvette?" Jacob called from the doorway.

"I've found it," she cried. And then with tears of relief in her eyes, she went to join him and said, "Let's go. It's time to reverse this spell."

## CHAPTER 11

Jacob stood in the middle of Hollow Books, watching as Yvette paced.

"I just don't know what she meant," Yvette said in frustration. "Marylin said that when we found the broom, we'd be able to reverse the curse. Well, I have the broom and I have the book. What exactly am I supposed to do now?"

That was the million-dollar question, wasn't it? He didn't know what to do. He hadn't even been there when Marylin had given her that tip. He'd been tied to a bed, staring down evil.

Yvette opened the book, placed it in the middle of the floor, and then laid the broom on top of it.

Nothing happened.

"Let's try something else," Jacob said.

Yvette whirled around to look at him. "Like what?"

"If we want to reverse the curse on Keating Hollow, maybe we need to go to the heart of Keating Hollow to do it."

"The river?" she asked.

He smiled softly at her. "No, love. To the Townsends. Text your sisters. Have them meet us at your dad's house."

Yvette didn't say anything at first, but then she slowly nodded and said, "Yeah, okay. It couldn't hurt, right?"

Jacob could think of a thousand things that could go wrong when trying to reverse a curse, but he kept those thoughts to himself. That was the last thing that Yvette needed to worry about. Besides, something deep in his soul told him that he was on the right track.

Once the text was sent, Jacob loaded his wife up in the car and hurried through town to the Townsend homestead.

The minute they pulled to a stop in the driveway, his two favorite people came running out of the house.

"Daddy!" Toby cried as he ran to his father and nearly knocked him down. "I thought you were never coming back."

Jacob chuckled. "We were just here this morning, little bud. Remember that?"

"It was too long ago." The little boy buried his face in Jacob's thigh and held on tight.

"He's upset because Grandma Clair wouldn't let him have a third cookie," Skye said with an air of superiority. "He cried for a half hour after she said no."

Jacob looked over the heads of his kids at Yvette, who was smiling down at them with limitless love in her eyes. Her complete devotion to their kids was one of the things he loved most about her. And even though Skye wasn't Yvette's biological daughter, she'd always treated her as if she were, and she was a far more stable presence in his daughter's life than Skye's biological mother had ever been. Of course, they'd adopted Toby, so the same could be said for him, though they didn't know his biological parents.

Whatever happened with the curse, he knew they'd find a way to survive it. If all they had was each other, it was enough.

Yvette's sisters started to arrive. And just like the last time the siblings tried to reverse the curse, Jacob, Clay, and Hunter got to work on making sure the pentagram and salt circle were ready for the Townsend sisters.

Then, holding on to both of his kids' hands, Jacob took a few steps back, giving the witches room to do their work.

Yvette placed the book and the broom in the middle

of the pentagram, and together with her sisters, she called on the goddess of spirit to reverse the curse. Magic lit up the property, swirling around like some sort of magical tornado. Yvette was illuminated with magic, looking more beautiful and ethereal than ever.

Jacob was in awe of her. The way she was in command of her magic, her pure determination to save not only her family's businesses, but the town, too. Her loyalty and dedication were unmatched.

Suddenly the magic stopped swirling. The book that was in the middle of the circle flipped open, and then the image of Kariann hovered over the book. Her dark curls were more unruly than ever. Her face was contorted in anger as her lips moved, but no sound came from her.

All five Townsend sisters stared at the image as if they were transfixed. Jacob wondered if they were caught in some sort of trance and was just about to do something, *anything*, to snap them out of it when the magic picked up again. This time when it stopped, Kariann was now holding the broom. She seemed to try to throw it down, but the handle appeared to be fused to her hand.

The apparition of Kariann jerked and swayed, appearing to try to get free, but nothing worked.

Finally, Yvette looked at her and said, "Reverse the curse. Free Keating Hollow from these unnatural binds. Release the curse, and we'll all be free."

The magic engulfed Kariann in a big ball of light and then shot right into the book. It slammed itself closed with a loud boom, the pillar candles that were flickering away at the Townsend sisters' feet snuffed out, and all the magic that had been filling the air vanished.

Yvette stepped forward, picked up the book, and smiled. "It's done. The curse should be gone." She turned the book so that Jacob could see the cover. The broom was back, and the witch that was holding it was none other than Kariann.

"Is that witch trapped in this book?" Abby asked.

"It looks like it," Yvette said. Then she pulled her four sisters into a hug, and Jacob could feel the love pouring off her. "Thanks," she whispered to them. "Never underestimate the power of the Townsend sisters."

Jacob's phone buzzed.

It was a text from Drew. *You better get down here. There's been a development.*

"Yvette?" Jacob called. "We need to go."

"Not yet, I—"

He shook his head. "It's Drew."

Yvette clamped her mouth shut, nodded once, stopped to talk to Clair, and then met him at the SUV.

They were both silent on the way to the station. As far as Jacob was concerned, he didn't really want to know the bad news. But when they turned onto Main Street, it was immediately clear that the spell was broken, and Yvette let out a loud whoop.

"It worked, Jacob. It really worked!" Her eyes were glistening with happy tears. "I hope this means the family businesses will stop blowing up, too."

"You can say that again." He opened the door to the sheriff's office for Yvette and followed her in.

Drew stood up from his desk and immediately waved at them to join him.

"What's wrong?" Jacob asked. "Did Kariann spell someone or get free?"

"That's..." Drew shook his head. "I'm not really sure what happened, but she said you two could help explain it."

Jacob shared a glance with Yvette, both of them skeptical.

But the minute they arrived at Kariann's—no, Marylin's—cell, Jacob understood the problem.

"She's gone," Yvette said.

"Right," Drew said with a nod. "The woman you brought me is gone, and now I have this completely different one, wearing different clothes. Someone needs to explain to me what happened."

Yvette grinned at him. "Kariann has been exorcised from Marylin's body, right Marylin?"

The strawberry blonde nodded as she matched Yvette's grin. "If you did it right, she's exactly where she should be, trapped in the pages of her book."

"Her book?" Jacob asked. "I thought you wrote it."

Marylin's expression turned cold when she said, "I did. But my sister cursed it out of jealousy. Shortly after it came out, anyone who read the spell aloud ended up cursed. I spent three years hunting down those books and doing my best to destroy them and help the victims reverse the curse. Ever since I learned about the curse, I've been calling it *her* book. She took all the joy out of it for me. I got to the point where I never wanted to see that thing again. I did my best to destroy all the copies I could get my hands on, but in the end, I kept one. Just one, to remind myself that sometimes dreams do come true. Even if they were sabotaged by my own sister."

Jacob felt sick. He couldn't imagine having a sibling who'd do such a thing. He thought of Yvette and her sisters and how they all had each other's backs, no matter the circumstances, and he felt so lucky to be a part of their family.

Yvette gave her a sympathetic look, and Jacob was sure she was thinking about her own sisters, too. Then she frowned and said, "There's a lot I don't understand. Like how did you two come to share the same body? And how did that book end up in my store?"

Marylin leaned forward in her cell and said, "Kariann came to live with me about a year ago. She was broke and on the verge of homelessness. Or at least she said she was. I'm not so sure, but either way, I couldn't just let her sleep on the streets."

"As any sibling would do," Yvette said.

The confined witch nodded. "Yeah, but she kept taking herbs from the garden, working on potions, and trying to invent new spells. One day a potion went terribly wrong, and she actually died. But as her soul was leaving her body, she managed to attach to me, and ever since then we've been fighting for dominance over this body." She waved a hand, indicating herself.

"Anyway," she continued, "that's how we ended up living together in both the house and my body."

"Okay, that explains the possession," Yvette said. "But what about the book?"

"That's easy. Kariann took it to your bookstore about a week ago and put it on a children's book endcap, hoping it would be picked up sooner or later," Marylin explained. "I tried to stop her, but she was too strong. Mostly I spent my days doing what she wanted. Always, except that one day she was trying out spells and knocked herself out. It was the strangest thing. I knew she was still there, but she was unresponsive. That's when I came up with a plan; if the curse was ever activated again, when it was reversed, Kariann was going right into the book, and I'd never have to deal with her again. So I spelled the book just in case."

"That kind of sounds like you wanted her to unleash

that curse on someone," Drew said from behind them. "That way you'd have a chance to get rid of her."

"You'd think so, wouldn't you?" Marylin asked amicably as if the sheriff hadn't just accused her of wanting a destruction curse unleashed on the world. "But no. The curse is too dangerous. In fact, Kariann even knew that I'd spelled it. I hoped it would stop her from messing with it, because a curse like that, no one is ever going to let it go. They will find out who is responsible, and they'll come knocking. Just like Yvette and Jacob did. Though, I do admit you came sooner than I expected. Well done." She mimed tipping a hat to them.

"Okay, so how did the book end up at Lincoln Townsend's house after the spell was cast?" Jacob asked.

"Magic. The book stays attached to the curse, so you must have called it or tried to reverse it," she said simply.

"And you're just innocent in all this?" Drew asked skeptically.

"Yes," Marylin said confidently. Then she bit her lower lip and said, "Well, except for the spell I cast that banished Kariann to the pages of the book. I bet that's not legal."

"It's not," Drew said, "but under the circumstances, we'll just let the MTF decide how to handle it."

Marylin gave him a grateful smile. "I think that's the best possible solution. They had no love for my sister."

Jacob knew that meant she wasn't going to serve any

time since Marylin was instrumental in bringing down someone they already had an eye on. He figured the agency would be happy to do what they could to keep her out of trouble.

"Excuse me," a male voice called from the waiting room. "Is Sheriff Baker in?"

"That's my cue," Drew said and left. A moment later, he returned with an agent from the Magical Task Force and said, "The agent wants to speak with Marylin privately."

"Sure," Yvette said as she joined Jacob.

He took her hand in his and started to lead her out of the holding area. But then he stopped and asked, "What happens to the book now that Kariann is trapped in it?"

Marylin gave them a cheeky grin and said, "I think it will look perfect on my bookshelf. Don't you agree?"

Jacob chuckled while Yvette worriedly bit down on her bottom lip. "What if someone takes it again?" she asked.

"Don't worry. I'll have it under lock and key. Sort of like the Hope Diamond. It won't be an issue ever again. I promise," Marylin said. "Trust me."

Jacob met the witch's gaze and just knew that there would be no safer place for Kariann than under Marylin's watchful eye. He kissed Yvette's temple and said, "I think we're done here."

She nodded. "Yes, we are. Let's get the kids and go home."

"I can't think of anything better." Jacob thanked Drew on his way out and then tucked his wife into the car. It had been the longest of days, and he wanted nothing more than to be home with his family, pretending none of this had ever happened.

## CHAPTER 12

Yvette stood in her store and felt her heart swell with love and pride as she watched the patrons line up to make their purchases. It had been two days since they'd broken the spell, and everything was already back to normal. The bookstore was doing better than ever. The parts for the taps had come in overnight, and Keating Hollow Brewery was on track to double its profits over last year's spring season. The spa's plumbing was fixed, and Hunter was already replacing everything that had been water damaged. They'd be up and running within the next few days. The insurance company had already settled Chad's claim over the break-in at the music store, and the wedding was back on, so Noel's inn was full again for the rest of the week.

"Did you ever find that footage you were looking for?" Brinn asked just after she thanked another customer and directed them to Incantation Café for coffee cake and lattes.

"I did," Yvette said. "It happened a week ago yesterday. Kariann, in the form of Marylin's body, walked right into the store and placed that book right there." Yvette pointed to the most prominent endcap. "Just like that, walked in, dropped it, and walked right back out. None of us ever saw a thing."

"It probably wasn't that hard to do if she came in on a busy day," Brinn said.

"Sure," Yvette agreed. But it still irked her. After Marylin had told her that the book was placed in her store, she couldn't stop thinking about it and had searched all her security tapes until she'd found it. She decided right then that she needed a bell on the door to tell them when customers were coming and going.

The bell chimed, and when Yvette glanced over, she spotted her husband standing there with a bouquet of sunflowers. Her lips curled into a slow smile. "Well, hello there, handsome."

"Hey, gorgeous," Jacob said as he walked over, handing the flowers to Brinn. "These are for you," he told her. "For being so generous."

Brinn flushed as she took the flowers. "You really didn't have to do this."

"I know, but you're covering for me so I can get my wife out of here for a while. It was the least I could do."

"You're what?" Yvette asked.

He held his hand out to her. "I heard you wished for a day for just the two of us. Maybe a ride up to the mountains?"

Warmth spread through Yvette's chest as she realized this was a surprise date. "Jacob Burton, are you trying to butter me up for something?"

His eyes flashed with mirth. "You bet. Are you game?"

"Just as long as we stay far away from Moonstone Ridge," she quipped.

"You got it. I think we've both seen enough of that place."

They certainly had, especially since the Magical Task Force had let Marylin go, and Jacob had gone with Drew to take her home. He'd said her house was gorgeous, magazine-level gorgeous, and that in addition to flowers being in bloom everywhere, the field was full of lavender, making it one of the prettiest places he'd ever seen.

While Yvette had been happy to hear that Marylin was free of her sister's ugly destruction, it wasn't a place she wanted to revisit anytime soon. Even if it was deemed the prettiest garden in the state, she was going to stay far away. She'd already seen enough.

"How about we head to the beach instead?" Yvette offered.

"There is a mountain that direction, too," Jacob said, pulling her closer to him. "I bet the kids would love it."

"The kids are coming with us?" she asked, her heart nearly exploding.

"Yep. It's family day," he said with a wink.

Yvette threw her arms around him and said, "You know what, Jacob Burton?"

"What?"

"I love you more today than the day I married you. Now let's go. The kids are waiting."

"Just one second," he said. Then he pulled her in close and dipped her dramatically before he whispered, "I love you too."

Yvette stared up into his gorgeous eyes and decided that no matter what this life threw at them, she was more than grateful that she got to navigate every day with the love of her life. "Good, now I hope you packed snacks."

Jacob just laughed and tugged her out of the store. When they got to the SUV, he opened her door for her and waved at the latte and coffee cake that was waiting for her. She grabbed him to her, kissed him thoroughly, and thought, *I married the perfect man.*

# DEANNA'S BOOK LIST

**Witches of Keating Hollow:**
Soul of the Witch
Heart of the Witch
Spirit of the Witch
Dreams of the Witch
Courage of the Witch
Love of the Witch
Power of the Witch
Essence of the Witch
Muse of the Witch
Vision of the Witch
Waking of the Witch
Honor of the Witch
Promise of the Witch
Return of the Witch

Fortune of the Witch
Song of the Witch
Rise of the Witch

**Keating Hollow Happily Ever Afters:**
Gift of the Witch
Wisdom of the Witch
Light of the Witch
Spell of the Witch

**Witches of Befana Bay:**
The Witch's Silver Lining
The Witch's Secret Love
The Witch's Lost Spell
The Witch's Hidden Garden

**Witches of Christmas Grove:**
A Witch For Mr. Holiday
A Witch For Mr. Christmas
A Witch For Mr. Winter
A Witch For Mr. Mistletoe
A Witch For Mr. Frost
A Witch For Mr. Garland
A Witch For Mr. Bell

**Premonition Pointe Novels:**
Witching For Grace

Witching For Hope
Witching For Joy
Witching For Clarity
Witching For Moxie
Witching For Kismet

**<u>Miss Matched Midlife Dating Agency:</u>**
Star-crossed Witch
Honor-bound Witch
Outmatched Witch
Moonstruck Witch
Rainmaker Witch

**<u>Jade Calhoun Novels:</u>**
Haunted on Bourbon Street
Witches of Bourbon Street
Demons of Bourbon Street
Angels of Bourbon Street
Shadows of Bourbon Street
Incubus of Bourbon Street
Bewitched on Bourbon Street
Hexed on Bourbon Street
Dragons of Bourbon Street

**<u>Pyper Rayne Novels:</u>**
Spirits, Stilettos, and a Silver Bustier
Spirits, Rock Stars, and a Midnight Chocolate Bar

DEANNA'S BOOK LIST

Spirits, Beignets, and a Bayou Biker Gang
Spirits, Diamonds, and a Drive-thru Daiquiri Stand
Spirits, Spells, and Wedding Bells

### Ida May Chronicles:
Witched To Death
Witch, Please
Stop Your Witchin'

### Crescent City Fae Novels:
Influential Magic
Irresistible Magic
Intoxicating Magic

### Last Witch Standing:
Bewitched by Moonlight
Soulless at Sunset
Bloodlust By Midnight
Bitten At Daybreak

### Witch Island Brides:
The Wolf's New Year Bride
The Vampire's Last Dance
The Warlock's Enchanted Kiss
The Shifter's First Bite

### Destiny Novels:

Defining Destiny
Accepting Fate

### Wolves of the Rising Sun:
Jace
Aiden
Luc
Craved
Silas
Darien
Wren

### Black Bear Outlaws:
Cyrus
Chase
Cole

### Bayou Springs Alien Mail Order Brides:
Zeke
Gunn
Echo

# ABOUT THE AUTHOR

New York Times and USA Today bestselling author, Deanna Chase, is a native Californian, who now splits her time between New Orleans and the Pacific Northwest. When she isn't writing, she is often goofing off with her husband, traveling, or playing with her two dogs. For more information and updates on newest releases visit her website at deannachase.com.

Made in the USA
Monee, IL
15 July 2025